#2

Weather's Here, Wish You Were Great

Don't get stranded.
Read all the books in the Castaways trilogy:

#1 Worst Class Trip Ever

#2 Weather's Here, Wish You Were Great

Coming soon:

#3 Isle Be Seeing You

From Aladdin Paperbacks
Published by Simon & Schuster

Weather's Here, Wish You Were Great

By
Sandy Beech

Aladdin Paperbacks
New York   London   Toronto   Sydney

ALADDIN PAPERBACKS
An imprint of Simon & Schuster Children's Publishing Division
1230 Avenue of the Americas, New York, NY 10020
Text copyright © 2005 by Catherine Hapka
Illustrations copyright © 2005 by Jimmy Holder
All rights reserved, including the right of reproduction in whole or in part in any form.
ALADDIN PAPERBACKS and colophon are registered trademarks of Simon & Schuster, Inc.
Designed by Tom Daly
The text of this book was set in Golden Cockerel.
Manufactured in the United States of America
First Aladdin Paperbacks edition July 2005
2 4 6 8 10 9 7 5 3 1
Library of Congress Control Number 2004109006
ISBN 0-689-87597-5

Weather's Here, Wish You Were Great

ne

Some people spend their whole lives dreaming of a long visit to a remote tropical island. They yearn to forget the hour on the clock and the date on the calendar, to live only by the timeless native rhythms of sand and sea.

Yeah, right. Talk about a nightmare!

"I think we could eat it," Ned Campbell said hopefully. The "it" in question was a many-legged sea creature my little brother, Kenny, had just dropped on the sand near the fire pit. It was crawling around in circles,

obviously confused by the strange forest of sunburned legs surrounding it.

Ryan Rodriguez leaned in for a better view. "It looks almost like a regular crab, but smaller."

Ned nodded and licked his lips. "Actually, I think it looks more like a crawfish or something—those are awesome, especially if you have some melted butter. . . ." He swallowed hard, probably choking back the drool building up in his mouth. Ned loves food. Any kind of food.

I wiped the sweat out of my eyes with the back of my hand and stared at the wriggling creature, which Kenny was calling a sand crab. About the size of an extra-large garden spider, the crab was the pale, watery beigy-yellow color of dried snot. It also seemed to have a few too many legs, though I couldn't be sure since it never held still long enough for me to get an accurate count.

"I don't know," I said dubiously. "I mean, I like a nice seafood meal as much as the next girl, but that thing looks like an extra in a horror movie."

I glanced at the others gathered around Kenny and the crab. It was midday, which meant the beach was hotter than a gorilla's armpit. Most of the group had disappeared right after lunch, probably to wander about in the

shady, relatively cool jungle interior or take a nap in one of the rocky caves in the cliffs along the beach. Only Ned, Ryan, and Brooke Hubbard had come wandering over in response to Kenny's triumphant cry of discovery a few minutes earlier. And me, of course. Don't ask me why. I should have known from experience that he'd just found some new kind of creepy crawly creature. Collecting bugs and reptiles—the uglier the better—is Kenny's third-favorite hobby. In case you're interested, number two would be watching cartoons on TV. Number one? Embarrassing me. It's practically his calling in life.

"I think it's totally gross," Brooke declared, staring at the sand crab with disgust on her strangely mottled face. Have you ever seen a dark-skinned African American with, like, fifth-degree sunburn? It's not a pretty sight. "You guys can eat it if you want," Brooke added, scratching a weltlike mosquito bite on her leg. "I'll stick to papayas, thank you."

Kenny shrugged. "That's okay. If you all don't want to eat these guys, I can add them to my zoo." He smiled eagerly at us, his eyes lighting up in his grubby face. "Did I tell you guys I'm building a zoo? It's in this clearing up on the mountain, and—"

"A zoo," I muttered, cutting him off. "Yeah, brilliant use of energy, Junior Einstein. A zoo is exactly what we need."

By the way, my name is Dani McFeeney. I used to be a pretty typical sixth grader. Popular, but not too popular. Smart, but not too smart. My grades have never been exactly perfect or anything, but I'm a reporter for the school paper, and the only sixth grader on the varsity basketball team. If you asked my two best friends, Michelle and Tina, to describe me in three words, Tina would probably say something like loyal, talkative, and competitive. Michelle might choose smart, fun-loving, and athletic. See what I mean? Typical girl, typical friends, typical life.

That was before my science teacher, Mr. Truskey, announced that he was taking ten of us Tweedale Middle School kids on a trip to clean up an old trash dump on some obscure island near the equator. Helping the environment while scoring a free tropical vacation on school time? It seemed like a great idea at first, and I was quick to volunteer. Too quick. It wasn't until I was committed that I realized Michelle and Tina had no interest in going . . . and that the most evil, repulsive, and snooty person in the sixth grade—or

4

possibly the entire world—had already signed up.

Saying that Angela Barnes and I don't get along is like saying the Hatfields and the McCoys weren't the best of pals. We've been mortal enemies pretty much since the first time we laid eyes on each other in first grade. Once we hit about fourth or fifth grade, we stopped most of the immature pranks—the garter snakes in her desk, the embarrassing pictures of me posted on the school bulletin board—and started just keeping out of each other's way as much as possible.

That's why, as soon as I found out Angela was going on the island trip, I did my best to get out of it. Unfortunately my parents decided it was the perfect time to teach me an Important Life Lesson about the value of following through on my commitments. Or something like that. I couldn't hear their lectures too well over my own wailing and gnashing of teeth.

Before I knew it I was sweating like a pig, scratching about a million mosquito bites, and trying to hold my breath a little longer each time I used the disgusting communal latrine. Oh, and spending ten hours a day lugging moldy old trash alongside Evil Angela. Talk about disgusting . . .

Castaways

Does all that sound like the bad part? No way. Compared to what came next, that part was like some kind of kittens-and-puppies-and-chocolate-sundaes paradise.

But to understand why, first you have to know about the choo-choo bug. That's the common name of an insect called the lesser equatorial beachwalker beetle, which is some kind of superendangered species. At least it's endangered in most of the world. On that particular island, choo-choo bugs were as common as pigeons in New York City. And almost as large.

The local choo-choo bug population was the main reason Mr. Truskey and his enviro-pals wanted to turn the island into a wildlife refuge in the first place. When we all got our first close-up look at a choo-choo bug, most of us wondered why anyone would want to save them at all. The critters are big, ugly, and active—sort of like a palmetto bug that got struck by the laser beam from a science-fiction movie and grew to three times its usual size. They also bite. A lot. By the time I'd been on the island an hour, I already had a huge, itchy welt on my ankle and two on my arm. They didn't exactly seem all that endangered to me, either—in the four days we spent cleaning up the island I became personally

acquainted with, oh, about half a million of them.

But according to Mr. Truskey, the bugs would be in danger if the island didn't get cleaned up, and that would be bad because they're an important part of the ecosystem, not to mention a big part of the local culture in the Esparcir Islands, the huge island chain where Trash Dump Island is located. Some of the native tribes even eat them. On the last evening of our cleanup trip, some tribe members from a neighboring island came to thank us with a big bonfire and cookout. The fish and vegetables they made us were pretty tasty, but when they offered up a final course of barbecued choo-choo bug, everyone said thanks, but no thanks . . . except Mr. Truskey. For some reason he decided that popping a huge, charbroiled insect into his mouth—legs, pincers and all—was a good idea.

But it wasn't a good idea. It was a bad idea. Very, very bad. Not only did it cause him to barf up everything north of his knees the next morning on the boat back to the mainland, it also sent his sanity lever swinging over from *mildly nuts* to *frothing-fruit-bat crazy.* I guess you could call it Montechoochoo's Revenge.

Before any of the rest of us realized quite how bad it

was, Mr. Truskey managed to steer our boat in the exact wrong direction before finally collapsing, puking all over the place, and passing out. We tried to take over and find our way back to the mainland, but instead wound up impaling our boat on the coral reef of a whole new island. The boat sank, we did our best to get ourselves and everything we could carry to shore, and that was it: We were stranded.

At first it didn't seem like a huge deal. Our other science teacher, Ms. Watson, had gone back to the mainland early with a sick kid, but we figured she'd come looking for us as soon as we failed to turn up on schedule. Then we realized a couple of important things: First, we were probably miles and miles from where she would start looking. Second, the weird wind patterns over the Esparcir Islands make it too dangerous to fly a helicopter, which meant the search party would have to travel by boat. There was no way of telling how long it might take them to find us. In the meantime all we could do was wait—and try to survive the heat, the boredom, and one another.

So that was how we ended up in our tropical island paradise. Some dream come true, huh? Oh yeah, and I

almost forgot to mention—there were choo-choo bugs on the new island too.

Anyway, after four or five days the food supplies we'd salvaged from the shipwreck were running low, so food was on our minds pretty much all the time. Luckily we'd already located a papaya grove and several large coconut palms, and the picture-postcard-blue water of the lagoon provided all the fish we could catch, so we weren't in any danger of actually starving. But by day five we were all seriously craving some variety in our diet. Hence our fascination with the colony of ugly little sand crabs my brother had found.

"I say we should at least try one," Ryan said, reaching over to poke at the creature again. It instinctively tightened its pincers, grasping Ryan's finger tightly. "Ouch! Hey, this thing stings!" Yanking his finger away, he stuck it in his mouth. He immediately made a face, removed the finger, and spat onto the sand. "Yuck!" he exclaimed, dancing around like a demented marionette. "That thing tastes like day-old butt."

Ryan is one of those people who would make an over-caffeinated howler monkey seem calm by comparison. My parents like to complain that I don't always think

before I speak or act, but that's only because they don't know Ryan. I'm not sure his brain is even connected to his mouth.

"You probably tasted the venom." Ned was still staring hungrily at the crab. "I'm sure it'd taste better once we cooked it."

Just then Mr. Truskey staggered out of the jungle, clutching a raggedy piece of bark in one hand and a long twig in the other. His longish black hair, which sticks up wildly in every direction even at the best of times, now resembled a nest of brawling Persian cats. There were twigs and leaves stuck in it here and there, and I think a small tropical bird had been trapped somewhere near his left temple for a while.

"People!" he cried when he saw us, squinting in the bright sunshine. "Splendiferous news! I've reached a breakthrough in my pepic . . . peptic . . . er, epic poem, 'The Rime of the Ancient Choo-Choo Bug.'"

"That's great, Mr. T," I called, forcing a smile.

He cleared his throat and held up the piece of bark as if reading from it, though all that was visible on it were a few random scratches. "'It is an ancient choo-choo bug,'" he recited with great solemnity. "'And it biteth one

of three. By my sunburned skin and dirty feet, now wherefore biteth thou me?'" He looked up and smiled at us. "Well, what do you think?" he asked proudly.

"Sounds awesome, Mr. T," Brooke said. "Um, very catchy."

"Ah, thank you, thank you . . ." As he staggered back into the shade, muttering and scratching at the bark with his twig, we all exchanged a worried look. Mr. Truskey didn't seem to be getting any worse, exactly, but he wasn't getting any better, either. How long did the effects of choo-choo poisoning last, anyway?

"That settles it," Brooke said firmly. "We're not eating anything we can't definitely identify. None of us," she added with an extra-stern glare at Ned.

I thought about pointing out that Brooke wasn't our leader—not anymore. At first she'd pretty much appointed herself dictator, partly because she was the only eighth grader on the island, but mostly just because she's bossy. The rest of us had rebelled after about a day and kicked her out, a fact she occasionally seemed to forget. But in this case it didn't matter, since I totally agreed with her.

"She's right," I said. "As co-vice-leader of this island, I say we forget about eating these things."

Ned sighed sadly. "What a waste," he murmured.

"Not necessarily." Ryan swooped forward and grabbed the sand crab again, this time ignoring its grabby pincers as he flipped it over in his hand. "This thing may not look much like food. But you know what it does look like?"

The rest of us stared at him blankly, but Kenny grinned. "Bait!" he crowed.

Ryan grinned back. "Good call, little dude," he said. "Come on, show me the rest of 'em. Then let's go fishing!"

I watched as the two of them raced off down the beach. "Guess that settles that," I said. "It's a good idea, actually. Maybe they can catch some bigger fish with those things."

It felt a little strange to be praising one of Spastic Ryan's ideas. Not quite as strange as it would have felt a week earlier, though. It was amazing how much Ryan had changed since the shipwreck. Suddenly the kid who usually managed to turn his homework into a paper airplane before he handed it in—if he remembered to do it at all—was putting his boundless energy to good use catching fish, gathering firewood, and hauling water from the stream.

He wasn't the only one who was surprising everybody either. Macy Walden, a shy, geeky seventh grader who

dressed like a refugee from *Little House on the Prairie*, was an absolute whiz at cleaning fish with a pocketknife. Even Ned was turning out to be amazingly useful. He might not have much firsthand experience with weather, being that it usually takes place outdoors and he prefers to stay indoors most of the time himself, usually watching TV or surfing the Internet. But he knows a lot about it. You know all those adults who say too much TV rots your brain? Well, if it's true, then Ned must have started out as some kind of supergenius, because his TV-rotted brain manages to hold on to all kinds of practical information and helpful hints from the Web, the Weather Channel, and who knows where else.

On the other hand, certain people weren't that different at all. . . .

My eyes narrowed as I saw Kenny slip several sand crabs into his shorts pocket when Ryan's back was turned. No surprises there. He wouldn't be the Kenny I knew and was forced to tolerate if he didn't have at least a few disgusting things in his pockets. No matter how much he sucked up to the others, he was still the same obnoxious little twerp who'd plagued my life since the day he was born.

Castaways

Oh, and why was my runt of an eight-year-old brother on a middle school trip in the first place, you ask? Excellent question! I suggest you pose it to the responsible parties, my parents. Apparently they cared more about having a "vacation from parenthood" (whatever that means) than about their only daughter's happiness and sanity. But that's another story.

Being stuck on the island with Kenny was about as much fun as a trip to the dentist. But that was nothing compared to the true, enduring misery that was life with Angela Barnes.

"Oh, Josh!" a loud, giggly voice rang out at that moment. "You're so funny!"

Turning around, I saw two people step out of the jungle. Angela's blond hair gleamed in the sun, and her big blue eyes were tilted up to gaze adoringly at the cute, dark-haired guy beside her.

I had found many, many, many reasons to despise Angela over the years. Since being stuck with her on the island, I'd discovered yet one more: Josh Gallagher.

Josh is one of those guys everybody likes. Everybody. The kids think he's cool, even though the teachers adore

14

him. He's in seventh grade, but the sixth graders aren't afraid of him and the eighth graders treat him like an equal. He's a starter on the boys' basketball team, so the jocks consider him one of their own, but the antijocks still like him too.

And then there's Angela. I'm pretty sure she had a crush on Josh even before the island trip. Being stranded with him just gave her an excuse to spend twenty-four hours a day drooling over him and trying to get him to notice her.

I wasn't about to make that easy for her if I could help it. Josh deserved better than Evil Angela. Way better. Leaving him in her clutches would be like encouraging him to dive into a pond full of hungry crocodiles. Maybe worse. At least the crocodiles wouldn't make him suffer for long.

I hurried over as they wandered in the general direction of the supply cave. Angela looked less than thrilled at my approach.

"Oh," she said. "What do *you* want?"

I smiled sweetly in response to her obnoxious question, not wanting to stoop to her level in front of Josh. "I was just coming over to see what's up," I said cheerfully.

"I thought maybe you were about to start a meeting or something. Why else would my two coleaders be hanging out together?"

Did I forget to mention that part? See, when we overthrew Brooke's reign of tyranny, we held a vote to elect a new leader. Angela and I were supposed to be the only candidates, but somehow almost everyone wound up voting for Josh instead. Talk about embarrassing! Then Josh said he'd only take the job if Angela and I would be his co-vice-leaders. That meant I was stuck spending way too much time with the Evil One as we attempted to figure out how to keep everyone happy and alive until whenever Ms. Watson got around to rescuing us.

Josh smiled back at me, not seeming to notice Angela's snotty behavior. He's polite like that. "Angela had a cool idea," he said. "She thought we should follow the stream back into the jungle and see if maybe there's some kind of spring at the other end. That way we might not have to boil all our water to make it safe to drink, you know? So we followed it for, like, half a mile just now. We didn't make it all the way to the source this time, but we did find a cool waterfall where the stream comes down from the mountain."

Weather's Here, Wish You Were Great

Glancing up toward the craggy hills that rose steeply in the center of the island, I nodded. As much as it pained me to admit it, even to myself, Angela's plan made sense. Even though it was probably just her devious way of setting up a private trek through the misty rain forest with Josh.

"Sounds cool," I said. "Maybe we can all go check it out before dinner. It would be nice to have, like, a real shower for a change."

"As if." Angela wrinkled her nose. "Just what we need—your grungy BO poisoning our only water supply."

I felt my cheeks grow hot under my sunburn. "Right," I replied sarcastically. "And I suppose you think you smell like a garden of roses right now yourself?"

Angela tossed her blond hair, which even I had to admit looked amazingly clean under the circumstances. "At least I try to keep myself looking human," she said coolly. "Just because we're stuck on this island doesn't mean we have to turn into total savages who've never heard of a hairbrush. Or soap." She gazed pointedly at my bare legs, which were streaked with dirt and sand.

"Okay, okay," Josh said weakly, sounding uncomfortable. "I'm sure we all wish we'd brought a little more shampoo on this trip, but—"

Angela didn't let him finish. "*I* certainly do," she said. "And more deodorant, too. Because then I'd have enough to share with Dirty Dani here."

I wasn't about to let her get away with that kind of comment—especially in front of Josh. "Oh yeah?" I retorted. "My legs might be a little sandy, but at least I don't have to bleach my hair blond to get people to notice me."

Okay, so maybe I sort of made that up. As far as I knew, Angela's hair color was one of the few nonfake things about her. But the important thing was that it worked. Angela's face turned such a bright shade of red that I was afraid her head might explode. No wait, not afraid; what's the other word? Oh yeah . . . hopeful.

"Come on, you guys." Josh seemed a little embarrassed by all the personal-hygiene talk. "We're all kind of grubby right now, but it's not like we need to be ready for, like, class pictures or a school dance or anything."

Angela gasped. For a second I thought she'd suddenly realized she was making a huge jerk of herself in front of Josh.

I should have known better.

Weather's Here, Wish You Were Great

"Guys! Guys!" she shrieked at the top of her lungs, sounding like one of the screeching jungle birds that woke us up every morning. She hurried down the beach toward the fire pit. "Hey, everyone, come here. I just had a great idea!"

"What's that all about?" I muttered suspiciously as I watched her legs flying over the sand as if she was racing for the last spot in the Miss Preteen Priss Pageant. Angela isn't usually the type to run when she doesn't have to. She prefers to move slowly so everyone has a chance to watch and admire her perfection. Or what passes for perfection in her deluded little mind, anyway.

Josh shrugged, looking as clueless as I felt. "No idea," he said. "Let's go see."

We drifted down to join the crowd gathering around Angela. Ryan and Kenny had already dropped their fishing pole and rejoined Brooke and Ned near the fire pit. Chrissie and Cassie Saunders appeared at the edge of the woods and Macy emerged from the supply cave.

Once she was sure she had everyone's attention, Angela finally continued. "Listen, Josh and I were just talking," she said eagerly. "Thanks to all our hard work, we're

totally rocking this island. We have tons of food, our shelter is awesome, and our rotating work teams are doing great."

I rolled my eyes. The election was over. So why was she still giving campaign speeches? I knew she was desperate for attention, but this was ridiculous.

"Anyway," Angela went on, "that made me think of an awesome way to pass the time while we're waiting to be rescued. We should have a beach dance!"

Two

I glanced around, ready to let the eye rolling commence. I was sure the others would be as underwhelmed by Angela's so-called brilliance as I was.

"Hmm," Brooke spoke up first, sounding intrigued. "A dance? But how? We don't have any music."

Cassie clapped her hands. "Yes we do!" she cried excitedly.

"Ned's radio!" her twin sister, Chrissie, squealed, sounding just as excited.

"Ooh! Good point." Brooke smiled.

I frowned. "Not really," I said. "All that comes in on

that thing is some salsa-music station, remember?"

Ryan grinned. "So what's wrong with a little salsa?" he asked, wriggling his skinny hips in what I guess was supposed to be his version of salsa dancing. "Sounds *muy fantastico*. Don't worry, Dani—I can teach you some moves."

I picked my jaw up off the sand, wondering exactly when the others had lost their minds. "You guys are kidding, right?" I said. "A dance? Get real. We have enough actual important stuff to worry about right now without something frivolous like that. Stuff like, oh, I don't know . . . *surviving*? Remember?"

Cassie looked slightly wounded as she answered. "We've been surviving just fine so far. Why not celebrate with a little party?"

"Yeah," Ryan put in. "We've been totally all-work-and-no-play for the past few days."

That much was true. I let my gaze wander around the beach. When we'd arrived it had been nothing but a blank stretch of white sand marking the space between surf and jungle. Now it looked almost civilized. Josh and Ned had designed our shelter, which featured a floor of smooth tree branches and a roof of palm boughs reinforced with tarps salvaged from the boat. Macy had used the little

sewing kit she had in her luggage, along with some fishing line, to sew the boat's life preservers together into a mattress. It was only big enough for about half of us to sleep on at one time, so we took turns—boys one night, girls the next—while the others slept on a pile of soft, but rather buggy and smelly, palm fronds. Someone had ringed the fire pit with rocks and shells, and there were enough logs set around it for everyone to sit down. Macy had even rigged up a sort of cook's workstation nearby. It was mostly just an old door from the boat, which we'd originally used as a raft when we abandoned ship, set on some large rocks and logs. But everyone agreed that it made slicing papayas and cleaning fish a lot easier.

We'd come a long way in just a few days, and we probably did deserve a little fun. But a beach dance with Angela in charge? To me, that practically defined *not fun*.

"Look," I said, choosing my words carefully. "Having some fun is a good idea. But this beach dance thing isn't our only option. Why don't we come up with some other ideas too, maybe take a vote on them?"

Angela totally ignored me. "Like I said, we're all surviving pretty well," she said to the others. "Besides, I'm sure Ms. Watson will find us soon—probably within the next

day or two. Why not try to have a good time until then? We could all use a break right around now."

What they could all use, in my opinion, was a good stiff dose of sanity. But as I glanced around the group, I could see that I was in the minority. Macy looked dubious about the whole thing, Ned was picking at his fingernails and looking bored, and Kenny had already lost interest completely and wandered off to check on the fishing pole. But Brooke, Ryan, and the twins were looking just as enthusiastic as Angela about the whole idea.

"I could wear that sundress I brought—it's still pretty clean," Cassie was saying eagerly.

Her twin nodded. "We could cook something special for dinner, spiff ourselves up a little. . . ."

"Right," Angela put in. "Josh and I just found this awesome waterfall—we could all take showers there."

I gritted my teeth. Did her evil know no bounds? I couldn't believe anyone was falling for her foolishness. It was completely obvious to me what this plan was all about—Angela just wanted an excuse to doll herself up and try even harder to get Josh's attention. Worse yet, I was afraid it might work. School dances and that sort of

thing were totally up Angela's alley. What if she managed to dissolve Josh's brains with her evil girly-girl powers?

I couldn't let it happen. I thought about pulling rank—my co-vice-leadership had to count for something, right? I glanced over at Josh, wondering if he would back me up. He was too smart and sensible to fall for Angela's dastardly plan, wasn't he?

He gazed back at me for a moment, looking thoughtful. "You know," he said to the group, "I guess this could work. A little fun and distraction right now might be exactly what we need. We could spend tomorrow getting ready, then have the beach party tomorrow night."

I just boggled. Seriously. I never really knew what that word meant before that moment, but now I do. It's when your brain sort of wriggles inside your head like it's trying to break out, but nothing else happens. No thoughts. No emotions. Just pure shock.

"Good plan, Josh," Angela said smugly. "How about it, everyone? Should we take a vote?"

I felt my heart sink into my sneakers as everyone else nodded. I'd had pretty bad luck with votes lately. But what could I say?

Castaways

"Um, what about Kenny?" Macy said softly. "Shouldn't we call him over before we vote?"

My little brother was still down near the surf line poking at something with a stick. I glanced at him, wondering how he would vote. He wasn't likely to be interested in any kind of party or dance—not unless it involved frog races or something. Then again, he might see it as an ideal chance to embarrass and humiliate me. And he might be right.

Brooke shrugged. "Kenny's too young to care about something like a beach dance," she said. "I think this time we can vote without him."

"I agree." Josh looked around. "Ready? Let's see hands up in favor of Angela's beach-party idea."

Angela's hand shot up immediately, while Brooke, Ryan, and the twins were just a split second behind her. Josh raised his hand too.

I glanced around frantically. As my gaze fell on Ned, I saw him shrug and lazily lift his hand to his shoulder. A second later Macy sighed and slowly raised her hand, looking nervous.

Before I quite knew what I was doing, I felt my own hand raising. Call it peer pressure if you want, but I didn't want to seem like a bad sport.

Weather's Here, Wish You Were Great

"Cool!" Angela sang out triumphantly, staring at me as if she knew exactly what I was thinking. I didn't think ESP was one of her evil powers, but you never know. "Looks like it's unanimous."

Ryan and the twins cheered. Macy and Ned shrugged. Angela continued to look pleased with herself.

Seeing that Josh was smiling as if this was actually a good thing, I did my best not to look as bummed out as I felt. But I couldn't help it; I had a bad feeling about this. My friends always dragged me to the school dances back home, but I usually spent most of my time there gossiping and trading jokes by the punch bowl, immediately cutting out to the bathroom whenever a slow song started. It's not that I don't like dancing, necessarily. I just didn't want to find myself turning into the type of girl I'd always despised—one of those makeup-wearing, eyelash-fluttering, boy-crazy girls who probably worship Angela Barnes as their queen.

As the others dispersed, most of them still chattering eagerly about the new plan, I sat dejectedly on my log. Ryan hopped up and came over to me.

"How about it, Dani?" he said, flinging his torso forward in what I guess was supposed to be some kind of

gallant bow. "Want to take me up on those salsa lessons now? By tomorrow night we could be the stars of the dance floor!"

I wasn't in the mood for his clowning around. "Not now, Ryan," I muttered. I stood up and brushed past him. "I have stuff to do."

That much was true enough. And the first thing on my agenda was figuring out how to handle this whole dance situation, which meant I needed some private time to think. Luckily I knew exactly where to go.

I grabbed one of the empty water jugs—my excuse, in case anyone tried to stop me—and headed into the jungle. Soon I was pushing my way through thick, drooping sheets of leaves that seemed to breathe out moisture at my touch, following the muffled sound of water tumbling over stone. A moment later I emerged into a small, sun-dappled clearing. The stream was narrow, deep, and twisty here; its bed was lined with rocks and pebbles and its banks were cut away sharply and spanned by tree roots here and there. Overhead an ancient-looking tree, much wider than it was tall, shaded everything with its gnarled, spreading branches.

I sighed, feeling a little more relaxed already. The place

where we all usually got water was about thirty yards upstream; I'd discovered this clearing on our third day on the island while searching for a shortcut back to the beach. It was already one of my favorite spots.

Leaving the water jug on the bank, I grabbed the tree's rough, flaky bark and hoisted myself up, clambering into its crook. I planted one sneakered foot on a knotted branch to balance myself and let the other dangle. Brushing away a choo-choo bug that was circling my head, I leaned back. The tree I was in made up only one of the many layers of foliage in the jungle, and I could glimpse only little bits of the sky through all the leaves and branches overhead as I stared upward and tried to figure out what was upsetting me so much about this whole beach-dance idea.

Why was it such a big deal? I absently picked at the bark of the tree with my fingers while picking at the question in my mind. It wasn't as if this was the sneakiest or most annoying thing Angela had ever done. It probably wasn't even the worst thing she'd done today. So why was it bugging me?

Bzzzz!

"Argh! Get away!" I muttered, waving my hands irritably

as the choo-choo bug I'd shooed away returned for another pass. It was kind of hard to think with a monster-size insect flapping around two inches from my face.

The ugly little creature buzzed just out of reach, then circled and returned yet again. A moment later a second choo-choo bug appeared, flying in from somewhere behind me.

I sighed, suddenly too tired and aggravated and gloomy to shoo them away. Instead I just watched as they circled around and around each other, their wings beating so fast they were almost invisible and their fat, shiny little bodies moving in a sort of . . .

"Dance," I murmured aloud. "It looks like they're dancing."

It was a pretty fanciful thought for me, and as soon as I said it, I was glad no one was around to overhear. I could just imagine what Kenny would do with material like that.

Still, it sort of felt like a breakthrough. Don't ask me why those two-stepping choo-choos finally made me see the light, but all of a sudden I sort of understood why I was so upset about the group's new party plans. Part of it was what I'd already known—I was sure Angela was going to use the beach dance to try to win over Josh,

30

maybe let him know for sure that she liked him.

But that wasn't the worst part. The worst part was what might happen next. What if it worked? What if Josh was won over by her blond hair and fluttering eyelashes? What if he decided he liked her back?

I shuddered at the thought. Being stuck on the island with Angela was bad enough. Being stuck there with a Josh-Angela couple? Pure torture. The smugness alone would be downright stifling.

No way could I just stand by and let it happen. My own comfort and sanity weren't the only things at stake, either. As Josh's friend I had to do my best to save him from her evil influence, whether or not he even realized he was in danger.

But how? I slumped back against the rough tree trunk, suddenly feeling helpless. Angela had been practicing the whole girly-girl act her entire life. All she had to do was blink her big blue eyes or shoot someone that prissy little smile, and she got whatever she wanted. My friends and I seemed to be the only ones immune to her powers. Poor Josh didn't stand a chance; at least, not unless I could come up with some kind of brilliant plan in the next twenty-four hours. . . .

Castaways

The choo-choo bugs whirred by again. This time I noticed that a third bug had joined them and was darting back and forth between them. As I watched, one of the original two let out an especially loud, irritated-sounding buzz and then flew off, leaving the other two together.

My eyes widened and I swallowed hard as I suddenly realized what I had to do. I stared into space, hardly aware that one of the choo-choo bugs had landed on my knee and was chomping into my skin. There was only one way I might be able to stop Angela from tricking Josh into liking her.

I had to try to get his attention myself.

Three

If my new plan was going to work, I was going to need help. I slapped at the choo-choo bug and jumped down from the tree. Brushing off my hands, I quickly grabbed the water jug and filled it before heading back to camp.

When I got there, I dropped the jug on the sand near the fire pit and then looked around the beach. Not a whole lot had changed since I'd left. Ryan and Kenny were fishing in the lagoon, with Josh joining in. Macy was using the small broom she'd made out of palm fronds to sweep up around the fire pit. Brooke, Angela, and Ned sat

in the shade of the supply cave. Mr. Truskey was barely visible wandering around at the far end of the beach.

I didn't pay much attention to any of them. Chrissie and Cassie were the ones I needed.

The twins were my best friends on the island. They're also probably the prettiest girls in the sixth grade—not that a certain vain and evil blond would ever admit that, of course. Thanks to their exotic, Asian-tinged features, flawless cinnamon skin, shiny black hair, and bubbly personalities, the twins have had boys falling all over them since the third grade. If anyone could help me figure out a way to distract Josh's attention away from Angela, it was Chrissie and Cassie.

I soon spotted them sitting together in the surf a few dozen yards down the beach, wearing matching red bathing suits. Hurrying toward them, I took a few deep breaths to prepare myself and calm my nerves. This wasn't going to be easy. If I wasn't very, very careful about how I explained things, it would be way too easy for the twins to jump to the wrong conclusions. And I definitely didn't want that to happen—not with Kenny and Angela lurking around, always eager for any chance to annoy and humiliate me.

Weather's Here, Wish You Were Great

Chrissie glanced up as I arrived. "Hey, Dani," she greeted me lazily, squinting against the afternoon sun. "What's up?"

"We were just talking about the dance," Cassie added, wriggling one leg to splash at the gentle waves rolling in over their laps. "It's going to be so cool, isn't it? I mean, it's not going to be like the dances back home or anything, but any dance is better than none at all, right?"

"No way," Chrissie said immediately. "A dance with, like, lepers or prison inmates or something wouldn't be better than none at all."

Cassie rolled her eyes. "Oh, please . . ."

"Wait!" I broke in quickly before they could get rolling. Chrissie and Cassie might look, sound, act, and dress alike. But that doesn't mean they always get along. Not even close. Unless you consider recreational arguing a hobby, in which case I guess they have that in common too. "I need to talk to you guys. It's about the dance."

I figured that would get their attention, and I was right. If Chrissie and Cassie had been choo-choo bugs, all of their antennae would have swiveled around immediately in my direction.

"What about it?" Cassie asked eagerly. "You mean you're

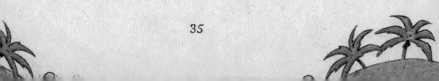

psyched too? We sort of thought . . ." She glanced at her twin uncertainly.

Chrissie shrugged. "We thought the whole thing was too girly for you," she said. "Especially because—well, you know. It being Angela's idea and all."

"That's sort of what I need to talk to you about." I swallowed hard, still only half-convinced that this was a good idea. "See, I think Angela came up with this whole dance idea just to, um, you know."

Two pairs of big brown eyes blinked blankly at me. "What?" Chrissie asked.

I shrugged, staring down at the foamy water lapping against the toe of my sneaker. "I think she's after Josh," I muttered in the general direction of my toe. "You know, like, romantically."

"Can't blame her for that." Cassie giggled and glanced down the shoreline toward the boys. Josh, waist-deep in the water, had just stepped forward to cast the fishing line while Ryan and Kenny watched. "He's totally hot."

"Yeah," Chrissie put in. "Like we'd say in Spanish class, *muy cállate.*"

Cassie frowned. "That's not right," she said. "It's *muy caliente.* I think *muy cállate* means 'very quiet' or something."

Weather's Here, Wish You Were Great

"No, it doesn't," Chrissie argued back, though she didn't sound too sure. "Where's Ryan? We could ask him."

"No!" I said, starting to feel a little desperate. How the heck was I supposed to pour out my secret innermost thoughts and plans if they wouldn't shut up for two seconds? "I want to go after Josh myself," I blurted out irritably.

Chrissie and Cassie gasped in unison. "No way!" Cassie cried.

"Shut up!" Chrissie shrieked gleefully. "You and Josh? How totally adorable is that?"

"Quiet!" I hissed. "*Muy cállate*, okay? I don't want the world to hear this." Suddenly the beach felt way too open and quiet. Macy and Mr. Truskey had disappeared from view by now, but the others were still around. And Kenny, for one, has hearing like a spy satellite. "Come on, let's go talk about this somewhere more private."

The twins hopped up and followed eagerly as I led the way across the beach and into the jungle. I passed the path to the stream, figuring we were too likely to be interrupted or overheard there. Instead I turned down the narrower path leading to our next-to-latest latrine. With eleven people using the same facilities—if you can

use a fancy word like *facilities* to describe a big, stinky hole in the ground—we were finding it necessary to dig a new latrine every couple of days. We'd abandoned this particular one just that morning in favor of a brand-new one some distance away down a different path. That made it the perfect spot for a secret meeting—especially one about a stinky subject like Angela Barnes.

I stopped at a wide spot in the trail just short of the stink zone, then turned and stared at the twins, feeling vaguely irritated, anxious, and embarrassed all at the same time. "Okay," I said. "First things first. I *don't* have a crush on Josh, okay?"

"What?" Cassie's face fell. "But you just said—"

"I said I want to get his attention. But that doesn't mean I like him or anything. I mean, I *like* him, I just don't *like* like him, you know?"

Chrissie shrugged, leaning against a tree trunk. "I guess. But if you don't *like* like him, why do you care if Angela is after him?"

"Because I like him," I replied. "Not like-like, just like. As a friend. I respect him too much as a person to let Evil Angela get her claws into him, that's all."

"Oh." Cassie shot her twin a long, meaningful glance.

Weather's Here, Wish You Were Great

I frowned, not liking that glance much. "You believe me, right?" I said. "Right?"

"Oh, sure," Chrissie said gleefully, tugging at the hem of her bathing suit. "Totally."

"Absolutely," Cassie agreed with a grin. "Why wouldn't we believe you?"

I could feel my face turning red. "Come on, you guys. I need your help, but if you're going to be stupid about this—"

"No, really." With some effort Cassie arranged her face into a solemn, sympathetic expression. "We totally want to help you sweep Josh off his feet and away from Angela's clutches."

"No matter what the real reason," Chrissie added mischievously. When Cassie elbowed her sharply, she quickly added, "which of course, is that you merely want to save Josh from Angela's evil slurping smoochy kisses. Totally on board with that. Definitely understandable. Really."

Annoyed that they weren't taking this more seriously, I opened my mouth to tell them to forget the whole thing. But before I could say a word, I heard a rustling from around the next curve of the path. Spinning

around, I saw Macy stepping into view with a slightly sheepish expression on her thin, sun-freckled face.

"Macy!" I blurted out, my face deepening into full-on Humiliation Red. "What are you doing here?"

She pulled nervously at the shoulder of her paisley-print blouse. "I was looking for my sun hat," she said in her soft voice that made almost everything she said sound like a tentative question. She held up a crumpled canvas hat. "See? I thought I might have left it at the old latrine yesterday, and I was right."

"Oh." My face still burning, I rapidly calculated the odds that she'd heard our conversation. It wasn't that I was worried about her spilling the beans to Josh or Angela—Macy wasn't that kind of person. Actually, I wasn't quite sure why I was so embarrassed. Before the trip I doubt I'd spent more than two minutes total talking to Macy Walden in my whole life, or more than five seconds thinking about her. She was just part of the scenery at school—the weird, slightly nerdy seventh grader with the overlong brown braids and the funny clothes.

So who cared if she'd overheard? Why did it matter if Macy thought I was some kind of Angela-esque girly-girl? I shouldn't give a flying choo-choo bug about her

opinion of me. But I was more than a little surprised to discover, all of a sudden, that I did.

Before I could ponder that any further, Macy cleared her throat. "I heard what you were saying just now," she said, her voice softer than ever. "Um, about Josh and Angela and everything."

"Listen," I began hastily. "It's no big deal. We were just, um, rehearsing a play we want to do at the party tomorrow night. It's called *Opposite Personality Day on the Island*, and—"

"No, it's okay, I understand," Macy broke in earnestly. "I think it's really great that you want to help Josh. He's too nice for someone like, you know, *her*."

I blinked, wondering if all that embarrassment had caused my brain to short-circuit or something. "Really?" I said cautiously. "I mean, um, yeah. That's exactly what I was trying to explain to these guys." I waved a hand in the twins' general direction.

Macy nodded. "Sorry about eavesdropping," she said. "It was an accident."

"No biggie." I glanced at the twins, feeling a little better about the whole situation. If Macy thought my plan was a good idea, how crazy could it be? "So how about it? Are you guys going to help me or what?"

41

"Totally," Cassie assured me. "We were just teasing before. We definitely want to help. Right, Chris?"

"Try to stop us!" Chrissie took a step toward me, looking me up and down like a tiger eyeing its prey. "Okay, so the first thing we need to do is figure out what you're going to wear tomorrow night."

"It has to be something really hot," Cassie put in. "I'm sure Angela will go all out, so Dani has to look totally off the hook."

Chrissie nodded thoughtfully. "Then there's the question of makeup. . . ."

I sighed loudly, wondering if I was getting in over my head by asking the twins for help. "Oh, yeah, this is going to be fun," I muttered.

"Don't worry, you'll do fine." Macy smiled at me. "Um, I'd like to help too, okay? You know, with your plans or whatever. If you want."

"Sure," I said, ignoring the twins' dubious expressions. Maybe Macy wasn't exactly a fashion plate. Or a makeup maven. Or a boy magnet. But she didn't want Angela to have Josh either, and that was what mattered. And for some reason, having her involved made me feel a little more optimistic about the whole thing. I smiled at all

three of my coconspirators. "I guess it's official, then. Operation Distract Josh is now in action!"

The four of us were discussing clothing options about ten minutes later when a whiny, droning, irritating sound interrupted us. No, it wasn't a swarm of choo-choo bugs. It was my dorky little brother.

"There you are," Kenny griped as he hurried up to us. "I've been looking all over for you guys."

"What do you want, loser boy?" I snapped. "We're busy."

Kenny ignored me, turning to stare at Cassie and Macy. "Angela's looking for you two," he said. "She says it's time to get back to work." He smirked. "Oh, by the way, all the work teams have new assignments."

The work teams were one of the ideas Josh, Angela, and I came up with once we became leaders of the island. Up until then, Brooke was ordering us around individually. If she told Ned to go get some water and then, fifteen minutes later, forgot she'd done that and sent Macy for water too, we ended up with too much water and no firewood at all. That kind of thing.

To make things more efficient, we decided to split everybody into three teams. We then divided all the regular

survival-type chores into three groups: food and water, shelter and latrines, fire and firewood. The three work teams took turns with the three chore groups, which kept anybody from getting bored or feeling like one team was doing all the dirty work.

We chose the teams by drawing names out of a big conch shell. The first team consisted of Angela, Cassie, and Macy. The next team was me, Brooke, and Ned. Josh, Chrissie, and Ryan made up the last one. We didn't include Mr. Truskey, of course—insect-addled nut jobs don't make the most reliable workers, and we figured he had enough to do just surviving his own insanity until we were rescued. We also didn't include Kenny. That part wasn't my idea—the little mutant gets out of enough chores at home thanks to his age, and I didn't think it was fair for him to get off easy on the island, too. But I was outvoted, thanks to the others' weird obsession with even numbers. Instead Kenny was assigned to be a sort of gopher for all the teams, helping out wherever he was needed.

"What are you talking about?" I asked him. "What new assignments?"

Kenny grinned at me. "Angela decided," he said. "She

probably didn't ask you because she figured she was smarter and prettier than you, so why bother."

I gritted my teeth. Kenny knows exactly how to press my buttons. And no wonder—he's spent his entire grimy little lifetime doing almost nothing else.

"Come on," I told the other girls. "Let's see what's going on."

When we reached the beach, we found everyone except Mr. Truskey sitting around the fire pit. Josh looked up when we came jogging across the sand at Kenny's heels.

"There you are," he said with a smile. "We were about to start a meeting."

"That's right," Angela said self-importantly, standing up and stepping to the edge of the ashy circle surrounding the fire. "I called it because we have important matters to discuss."

I entertained a fleeting fantasy of seeing her fall on her butt in the ashes. That would teach her to wear white shorts on a deserted island. . . .

Then I shook it off. This was no time to get distracted. The sooner Angela's silly meeting was over, the sooner I could get back to planning her humiliation and defeat.

"So spill it," I said. "What's the big emergency?"

Angela shot me a snooty glare. "I was just getting to that, if you'd switch off the motormouth long enough to let me finish." She looked around at the others. "See, I realized we're going to have to work hard if we want to be ready for our beach dance tomorrow night. So I think we should get started on the preparations right now."

Macy looked dubious. "Are you sure? We're almost out of firewood, and it will be time to start fixing dinner before long. . . ."

"Whatever," Angela said irritably. "It's not like we can't keep up with our normal chores too. But at the same time, we can be getting ready for tomorrow night."

"Makes sense, I guess." Ryan shrugged. "But how much is there to do, really?"

"Tons!" Angela's eyes widened dramatically. "We want this dance to be special, right?"

There was a vague mumble of various voices, best summed up as the general emotion *sure-whatever*. Angela scowled, looking more irritated than ever.

"Look, did we all vote for this idea, or what?" she demanded. "I don't want to be stuck doing all the work

here, okay? And I definitely don't want the dance to turn out totally lame."

Brooke nodded briskly. "She's right," she said with a hint of her old student-council-obsessed, pep-rally-loving, most-likely-to-succeed, rah-rah spirit. "If we're going to do this, we might as well do it right."

"So what do we need to do?" Cassie called out, raising her hand as if she were back in school.

"Good question, Cassie," Angela said, any hint of irritation gone now that she was getting her way. "I've already divided the tasks into three batches, just like we did with the chores." She smiled sweetly at Josh. "Josh and the rest of group A, you guys will be in charge of food. We'll want something special to celebrate the night, so be creative."

"Okay," Chrissie said eagerly, glancing at Josh and Ryan. "We'll come up with something awesome. Right, guys?"

"Totally!" Ryan leaped to his feet, grabbed a couple of coconuts from the pile near the food-prep table, and started juggling them. Or attempting to, anyway. "I'm practically a master coconut chef by now. It'll be a gastronomic masterpiece!" He ducked as one of the

coconuts almost beaned him on the head, causing the other one to bounce off his knee and roll into the fire.

"Okay, whatever." Angela ignored Ryan's antics as she pointed to Brooke, Ned, and me. "Group B, you'll take care of decorations."

"Decorations?" I exclaimed. "Are you kidding? How are we supposed to do that—run down to the Island Hallmark for some balloons and streamers?"

Most of the others giggled, though Angela didn't look amused. "Use your brain, Dani," she snapped. "It's that stuff inside your head that keeps your ears apart."

"Very mature," I said loftily. "I ask a reasonable question, and all you can do is insult me. So tell us, what are *you* going to be doing while I'm trying to create a disco ball out of seashells and choo-choo bugs?"

Angela pursed her lips. "My group is in charge of general planning," she said. "We'll take care of everything that's not covered by the other two groups."

"Like what, bossing people around?" I muttered.

But by then, nobody was listening anymore. Everyone was already scooting around, dividing into groups, and chattering excitedly about their tasks.

Brooke and Ned hurried toward me. "Listen, we don't

have much time before the dance, so we'd better get started on these decorations," Brooke said urgently. "Who has ideas?"

"I do," Ned said eagerly. "I saw this TV show once where somebody was getting married in Tahiti, and they made these cool garlands out of vines. . . ."

Four

"Geddawayfromme," I mumbled, waving my hand at the mosquito buzzing around my face. "I mean it. I'm not in the mood."

The mosquito seemed unimpressed as it continued buzzing. With a sigh, I hoisted my armload of thick, twisty vines over to my other shoulder and glanced upward. Even in the shade of the jungle, I was dripping with sweat after spending the last half hour gathering vines that didn't particularly want to be gathered. Brooke had loved Ned's garland-making idea, and they wanted to get started right away.

Weather's Here, Wish You Were Great

I figured twining a bunch of buggy vines together and drooping them around the place wouldn't be any worse than the pathetic crepe-paper-and-confetti decor of the average Tweedale Middle School dance. But it still irritated me to spend my time and sweat trudging through the jungle collecting vines when Angela's "general planning" group was probably sitting around sipping cool, fresh water while discussing, oh, I don't know … whether the beach dance should start at seven or seven thirty.

The very thought made me want to tie her up with one of my vines and dangle her over a nest of hungry choo-choo bugs. And just then I spotted the perfect vine for the task, dangling nearby. It was long, thick, and smooth, with bright green leaves sprouting out of it and picturesque tendrils here and there. As soon as I saw it, I knew Ned and Brooke would love it. The only trouble was, the vine was hanging down from way up near the top of one of the taller trees in the area, its other end lost from view in the misty canopy.

"This is stupid," I muttered, staring up at the vine. "Why am I doing this?"

I sighed and dropped the vines I was carrying, already knowing the answer to my question. I was doing it

because of Operation Distract Josh. Josh was a leader, a team player. If he thought I wasn't pulling my weight, I wouldn't have a mosquito's chance in Antarctica of impressing him.

Reaching up, I gave a tentative yank on the vine. It barely budged. All the Tarzans from all the bad B movies in Hollywood could have swung on that thing all day long without any danger of hitting the ground.

As I was wondering if I should go back to camp for a knife, I heard rapid footsteps coming down the path behind me. Glancing over my shoulder, I saw Kenny crash out of the jungle, wild eyed and red faced.

"Dani!" he panted when he spotted me. "Did you see a big green lizard with red eyes and yellow spots come this way? About this size?" He held up his hands in a position that indicated something about the length of a small golden retriever.

I wrinkled my nose. "Ew. No," I said. "And I hope I don't see it anytime soon, either."

Kenny looked disappointed. "Darn, I thought I almost had it," he grumbled, flopping down on the path and swiping one grubby hand across his brow, leaving a streak of sweaty dirt behind. "I really want to catch one

of those guys for my zoo, but they're super fast."

"Hmm." My attention was already returning to the vine. Maybe if I climbed the tree and tried to get at it from above . . .

"You should come see my zoo," Kenny chattered on, apparently already recovered from his disappointment in failing to capture Godzilla Jr. "I've got tons of animals there already. There are, like, fifteen or twenty different kinds of insects and seven kinds of spiders. . . . Well, I think I only have six now, since that big hairy brown one got away. . . ."

I chewed my lower lip, wondering if I should go look for Brooke and Ned. If they wanted this vine, they should have to help me get it. Meanwhile Kenny kept blabbing on and on, his voice almost as irritating as the mosquito that was still swooping around my head.

". . . and I've been figuring out how to build stronger cages for them so they'll stay put. I even caught two of those little mouse things we always see around camp, so I hope they might have babies," he said, sounding excited. "I'm going to fix up the rest of the cages and then start inviting people up to see it. If it's good enough, maybe I can charge admission."

The ridiculousness of his last comment broke through

my distraction. "Oh, yeah, right," I said with a snort. "Maybe if you save up a few bucks from that brilliant plan, you'll have enough cash to take in a movie down at the Island Cineplex."

"I wasn't going to charge actual money, *Duh*-nielle," he said, rolling his eyes almost all the way up into his head. He knows I hate when he does that—it grosses me out. "They can pay me with stuff that's useful here on the island. Like extra food, or trading chores, or whatever. Hey, if you talk some of the others into checking it out, maybe I'll let you in for free."

"Whoop-de-doo." I wasn't in the mood for Kenny's infantile projects. Even less than usual, I mean. "I just might have to pass on that fabulous invitation. The whole stupid zoo thing sounds boring with a capital yawn."

He frowned. "How do you know? You haven't even seen it."

"I don't have to see the planet Neptune to know it's not a good place to get a tan," I retorted. "I mean, who's going to want to pay so much as a rotten coconut to see a bunch of bugs and rats and snakes? We all see way too many of those things on this island as it is."

His face fell. "Whatever," he muttered.

He looked so crestfallen that for a second I felt sort of bad. Trying to make it up to him, I ventured a slight smile.

"Hey, but if you actually want to do something useful, you could help me out here," I offered in the friendliest voice I could manage. "Maybe if I lift you up to that crook in the tree, you could climb up farther and cut that vine down, and—"

"Forget it," he interrupted. "You can cut down your own stupid vines. I'm busy."

I sighed. Why did I even bother trying to talk to him like a human being? "Fine. Later, dork boy," I said, grabbing my pile of vines and heaving it back up onto my shoulder. Leaving Kenny glaring after me, I headed back toward camp.

A few minutes later I emerged squinty eyed out of the shady jungle onto the blazing-bright beach. I dumped my vines on the sand, then rubbed my tired shoulder and looked around.

"Oh, great," I muttered to myself when I noticed most of the others gathered around the fire pit. "Looks like I'm the only one actually working."

I wandered over to see what they were doing. "Hey, maybe Dani will have some ideas about what to do,"

Cassie said when she saw me. "Come here, Dani."

"I'm here." I flopped down on an empty log seat. "What's going on?"

Josh smiled at me. "The General Planning Committee has a dilemma on their hands."

"I wouldn't call it a dilemma," Angela said with a slight frown.

I thought about making some kind of crack about how Angela wouldn't use any word with that many syllables. But I restrained myself.

"What's the problem?" I asked instead, reaching for a water bottle nestled in the sand nearby and taking a long swig.

"Angela thought we should have a name for the beach dance," Macy explained. "The trouble is, we don't even know what this island is called."

Angela nodded. "But it's no big deal," she said quickly. "All we have to do is come up with a good name. And I already thought of one: Tropic Sunshine Island."

Ryan wrinkled his nose. "Are you kidding?" he said. "No offense, but that name sucks out loud."

"Oh, yeah?" Angela looked insulted. "I suppose you could come up with something better?"

Weather's Here, Wish You Were Great

"With my brain tied behind my back," Ryan bragged.

Josh held up his hands. "You know, I think we should talk about this a little more," he said tactfully. "Angela, I think your name is cool. But we should probably get suggestions from everyone and then hold a vote, okay? That's the fairest way to do it, don't you think?"

He smiled at her. His teeth are always pretty white, but they looked whiter than ever against his island-tanned skin.

Angela's expression remained stormy for about half a second before softening into a simper. "You're right, Josh," she agreed sweetly. "That's a great idea. I was just going to suggest it myself."

I shot the twins an "oh yeah right" eye roll. If anyone but Josh had suggested taking a vote, I suspected Angela's response would have been very different.

"Well?" Josh glanced around the group. "Any brilliant ideas?"

"How about Beachcomber Island?" Cassie called out.

Chrissie shook her head. "Too boring," she declared. "How about Nowhere Island?"

"No—Anywhere But Here Island!" I joked.

Ryan grinned. "Island of the Idiots!"

"Shipwreck Island!"

"Choo-Choo Island!"

People continued to shout out ideas, some silly and some serious. Macy was the first to notice the shambling, bewhiskered figure heading toward us from the jungle.

"Hi, Mr. Truskey," she called out.

The teacher lifted a hand in greeting. His gaze actually seemed to focus on Macy as he responded. "Hello, Maypole," he said. "Hello, people. What are you all doing?"

I stared at him in surprise. Ever since being struck down by the choo-choo crazies, he'd had trouble remembering pesky little details like our names. Even if he hadn't quite gotten Macy's right, it was a lot closer than usual. That seemed like a good sign.

I guess Brooke thought so too, because she responded to him as if he was actually sane. "We were just trying to come up with a name for the island, Mr. Truskey."

Angela nodded. "See, we're having this dance tomorrow night. . . ."

I didn't hear the rest, because Chrissie and Cassie suddenly grabbed me by both arms and pulled, almost yanking me off my log and into the sand.

"Come on," Chrissie whispered. "We need to talk to you."

Cassie gestured to Macy, who followed as we hurried away from the fire pit. Soon the four of us were standing just inside one of the many smaller caves that pitted the cliffs on either side of our supply cave.

"What's up?" I asked. "We shouldn't stay away too long or Angela's likely to bully the others into naming this place Angela-Barnes-is-Perfect Island or something."

Chrissie rolled her eyes. "Forget about that," she said. "Cass and I just thought we should have a meeting to see how things are going so far. So—anything new to report on Operation DJ, Dani?"

They all stared expectantly at me. "Nothing much in the last hour and a half," I replied sarcastically. "Give me another five minutes, and I'm sure things will be hopping."

Chrissie sighed. "Come on, Dani. If we want this plan to succeed, you're going to have to work a little harder at it."

"Doing what?" I was honestly perplexed. "It's not like I can hit him over the head and force him to worship me." I grinned. "Although that technique seems to work for Angela. . . ."

Cassie ignored my witty remark as she responded earnestly. "No, but you can start flirting and stuff. You

know, like charming him whenever you get him alone."

"I guess," I said dubiously. Even if such a thing were the-oretically possible, I had serious doubts about my ability to pull it off with a straight face. "But I haven't run into him alone since we came up with the plan."

The twins exchanged a disappointed glance. Even Macy looked worried.

"If the right moment doesn't happen on its own, you might have to create it," Chrissie said.

Cassie nodded so hard she looked like a bobble-head doll. "She's right," she said. "We're going to need to do some strategizing, maybe see if we can set up some kind of private moment between you two—"

"Hold on a second here." I was feeling more and more skeptical about this whole plan. "This is all starting to sound a little sneaky and two-faced. I don't want to start acting like Angela Barnes the Second."

"You won't be," Cassie said.

"Definitely not," Chrissie added.

Macy cleared her throat. I was sure she was going to agree with me—she's so honest it's scary. She would never approve of deceiving Josh even in a relatively minor way.

Weather's Here, Wish You Were Great

"Sometimes you have to fight fire with fire," she said softly.

I blinked at her in surprise as the twins nodded vigorously. "Angela's way ahead of you already," Chrissie pointed out. "She's been flirting like crazy since we landed on this island."

"Before," Cassie corrected. "Dani, you've got to get with the program."

"You need to step up your game."

"We have to have a plan."

Feeling outnumbered, I sighed and held up both hands in a gesture of surrender. "Okay, okay," I said, mostly just to shut them up. "I guess we can give it a try."

As we parted ways a few minutes later I was feeling a bit queasy, and it wasn't just because the twins' quick flirting lessons had made my stomach churn. At first Operation Distract Josh had seemed like just another prank—a goofy little secret way to keep Angela from getting what she wanted. But all of a sudden it was starting to feel more like a serious competition.

Don't get me wrong, I usually love to compete. Whether it involves a basketball court or a Monopoly

board, a spelling bee or a backyard watermelon-seed-spitting match, I always play to win. But this was one contest I wasn't too crazy about so far.

And a little voice inside me was whispering the reason why: It was because this was one contest I wasn't really sure I could win.

Five

I got my chance to be alone with Josh sooner than expected. I didn't even have to pull anything sneaky to do it.

"Stupid vine," I was muttering as I stared upward at the vine dangling in front of me, its moist green tendrils seeming to taunt me as it stubbornly refused to loosen its hold on whatever trunk or branch it was clinging to far overhead.

"Hi, Dani."

At the sound of Josh's voice behind me, I spun around

so fast I tripped over the latest pile of vines I'd collected, almost landing flat on my face. Graceful.

"Oh—hi," I said, my face growing hot as I wondered if he'd just heard me scolding a vine as if I was some kind of mental patient. Deciding that humor was the only thing that might get me out of that one, I smiled weakly. "Um, the vine and I were just having a little argument."

He smiled back. "I hope you were winning."

"Unfortunately, no." As my brain finally caught up to what was happening, I realized this was my chance. My stomach clenching nervously, I tried to recall what the twins had just told me about flirting. *Act interested in him,* Cassie had urged. *Ask him lots questions about himself.*

"So what are you doing here?" I blurted out. Too late I realized the question sounded a little threatening, which probably wasn't the mood I was going for.

Luckily Josh didn't seem to notice. "I'm looking for a patch of this certain kind of greens," he said. "Ned saw a TV show on tropical delicacies, and he's sure he spotted some edible stuff down by the stream. It's supposed to taste sort of like spinach or something. We thought we could fix it for the beach party and see if everybody likes it."

Be superenthusiastic about stuff that interests him. The twins'

voices floated through my mind. *Let him know you're impressed by what he's saying.*

"That's awesome!" I shrieked.

Josh blinked. "Um, yeah," he said. "We could definitely use some green vegetables in our diet, right?"

I let out a loud giggle. "You are *so* right, Josh," I gushed, feeling like the world's biggest dork. "You're really smart."

He was looking more confused with every goofy comment and psychotic giggle. "Are you okay, Dani?" he asked with concern. "It's pretty hot out here, and you seem a little, um, you know . . . Maybe you should sit down for a minute? I could go get you some water if you want."

Great. I go for an adorable coquette sort of thing and end up conveying heatstroke. "'S okay," I muttered. "I'm fine."

"Oh. Good." He still looked worried, but he didn't say anything else.

I should have known better than to try to act like the twins. Maybe they could carry off the giggly-flirty-girly act without looking like total losers, but it just wasn't me. There was an awkward moment of silence as I stared at Josh like Bambi in the headlights.

He stared back at me. "Listen," he began uncertainly. "About tomorrow night . . ."

I winced, wondering if it was possible to enforce a restraining order on a deserted island. Preferring not to find out, I searched my mind frantically for a way to fix things. I had to let him know—and fast—that I was still me. I was still the sane and normal person he knew from school and basketball practice, not some demented girly-girl Angela clone.

"Yo, what about it, dude?" I demanded in my best tough-jock, just-one-of-the-guys voice. I reached over and punched him on the arm.

"Ow," he blurted out, looking startled.

"Oops." I guess I'd punched him a little harder than I'd intended. "Sorry about that. Dude."

He shrugged, rubbing his arm. "No biggie," he said. "Anyway . . ."

His voice trailed off and he licked his lips, looking sort of nervous. And no wonder. I'd be nervous too if I was trapped in the jungle with me at that point.

I was almost relieved when I heard a way-too-familiar voice calling out Josh's name. Almost.

"Hey there, Josh!" Angela cooed, smiling at him as if he was the last parking spot at the mall. Then she glanced at me. "Hi," she added curtly. "Are you almost finished

out here? The rest of your team is looking for you back on the beach."

"That's nice," I said blandly, wondering how she always seemed to appear wherever Josh happened to be. Did she have some kind of homing instinct, like a horse that always knows its way back to the stable?

Angela slipped her arm through Josh's and smiled up at him. "Ned just told me you've been working superhard putting together a special meal for tomorrow night," she said. "That's so awesome—I'm glad you're getting into the spirit of this beach dance."

Josh glanced down at his arm, looking surprised and a bit uncomfortable to find it intertwined with Angela's. Then again, maybe that was wishful thinking on my part. Maybe he was relieved that she had showed up to rescue him. She might not have much of a personality, but at least she wasn't channeling multiple ones the way I seemed to be at the moment.

"Yeah, we're doing what we can," he said. "I just want the party to be as much fun as possible. It will be a good way to keep everyone's spirits up while we wait for Ms. Watson to show."

"Too cool," Angela purred, squeezing his arm even

tighter. "You're so thoughtful! No wonder everyone wanted you to be our leader." She tilted her head to one side and shot him a weird little half smile. "I'm sure everyone is dying for the chance to dance with you tomorrow night too."

"Yeah," I broke in, unable to restrain myself. "I'm sure Ryan and Ned are dreaming of nothing else."

Angela paid no more attention to my comment than she did to the multilegged insect crawling up a tree nearby. "So I figured I should get my request in early," she purred at Josh. "Will you promise to save the first dance for me, Josh? Please?"

"Um, sure," Josh mumbled uncertainly. He glanced over at me, probably wondering if I was even the same species as Angela.

I was sort of wondering the same thing myself. How did she do it? I couldn't even manage to put together a coherent sentence in Josh's presence, while she had just wheedled a dance out of him.

As I watched the two of them wander off down the trail together, one thing was clear to me. Operation Distract Josh was in trouble.

Big trouble.

Weather's Here, Wish You Were Great

* * *

I was still feeling humiliated and irritable when the twins found me on the beach an hour later. "Hey," Cassie said breathlessly, flopping onto the sand beside me. "How's it going?"

Chrissie sat down on my other side. "Did you totally distract Josh yet?"

"Depends on your definition of *distract*," I grumbled. "If you mean 'scare him,' I'm doing great so far. If you mean 'make him like me,' not so much."

Out of the corner of my eye, I saw them trading a surprised look as I leaned over the pile of vines in front of me. I was sitting on the firm, moist sand the most recent high tide had left in the middle part of the beach. That was where Brooke, Ned, and I had dragged most of the vines we'd collected. For the past twenty minutes, while the others went back for another pile, I'd been attempting to weave the long, slippery vines into garlands. It wasn't going very well so far, which hadn't done much to improve my mood.

"Hold the phone," Chrissie said. "Is there a problem?"

"A big one," I said. "I'm thinking this whole stupid Operation DJ plan was a huge mistake. Josh is a big

boy—if he wants to tell Angela to take a hike, he can open his mouth and do it. He doesn't need my help."

Cassie gasped. "No way!" she cried. "You'd be crazy to give up now! Tell her what you heard, Chris."

I suddenly noticed the giddy expressions on the twins' faces, which were somewhat different from their usual giddy expressions. "What did you hear?" I asked.

Chrissie grinned like a cat who'd just swallowed a whole flock of canaries. "Okay, well, I was just down in the cove gathering clams with Josh and Ryan," she said. She wrinkled her nose, which made her look like a particularly pretty pug dog. "Ew, I hope those things taste better than they smell. Because talk about gross . . ."

"Focus," I ordered, shoving away a vine that was tickling my ankle. "I assume this story has a point."

"Yeah, yeah!" Chrissie giggled. "So anyway, we started talking about different people on the island, and the two guys spent, like, ten minutes raving about how great you are."

"Really?" I said cautiously, still waiting for the punch line. "What did they say, exactly?"

Chrissie shrugged. "Well, I forget how it started." She raised one hand to her forehead as a sudden breeze sent

her dark curls bouncing over her eyes. "I think Ryan said something about how smart you were, and then Josh agreed, and then one of them said you would probably be a lot of fun at the beach dance—I think that was Ryan too, actually, but Josh looked really sincere when he agreed that time, and—"

"Dani, Dani, Dani!" My little brother's excited shout drowned out whatever Chrissie was going to say next. Glancing up, I saw Kenny racing down the beach toward us, barefoot and grubby as usual.

"What do you want?" I asked as he skidded to a stop in front of me. "Hey! Watch it," I added. "You're kicking sand all over my vines."

"Sorry." Kenny sounded breathless and distracted. "Guess what, you guys? I finally caught one of those lizards for my zoo!"

We all stared at him blankly. "Huh?" I asked.

"Remember, Dani? I was telling you how fast they are." Kenny gazed at me. "Remember? Come on, are you stupid or something? Don't you remember?" He was starting to look kind of agitated.

Kenny is even more of a pain in the behind than usual when he's agitated, so I nodded and pretended to know

what he was talking about. "That's nice," I said, climbing to my feet. "I'm sure you two will be very happy together. Why don't you tell these guys all about it while I go help my team bring out the rest of the vines?"

"But—," Chrissie began.

"Wait—," Cassie blurted out at the same time.

"Hey—," Kenny put in.

Before any of them could finish, I put all those wind sprints Coach Hammond is always making us do in basketball practice to good use and made my escape. "Be right back!" I called over my shoulder.

I felt a twinge of guilt about sticking the twins with Kenny when he was in full pest mode, but I figured I could make it up to them later. Right now I needed some time to think.

I slowed to a jog and then to a walk once I reached the shade of the jungle. The rational part of my brain knew that what Chrissie had just told me was supposed to be good news. If that was true, why did it make me feel strangely uneasy, as if a colony of ants was crawling around just under my skin?

Josh likes me.

I rolled the words around in my brain for a moment as I

Weather's Here, Wish You Were Great

wandered down the latrine trail. Could it be true? I had no idea. And suddenly, I wasn't even sure I wanted to know.

My face grew hot as I thought back to our encounter earlier that afternoon. How could someone like Josh have any interest at all in a total, irredeemable doofus like me? It just didn't seem possible.

But if it was . . .

Shaking my head impatiently, I wondered just exactly what was happening to me. Why did things always have to get so complicated? All I'd wanted to do when I started this was prove to Evil Angela that she wasn't as perfect as she thought she was.

Angela. In all the angst over Josh, I'd almost forgotten about her. The object of my repulsion.

Despite the tropical heat, a shiver ran through my body. When it came right down to it, it didn't matter what Josh really thought of me. I just had to win out over the Evil One. No matter what it took.

That night the orange and gold flames of the campfire were so bright that they left little dancing light spots behind when I blinked my eyes. Or maybe it was just that I spent about fifteen minutes straight gazing fixedly into

the fire while trying to psyche myself up for the following evening's epic battle between the forces of good—aka me, the twins, Macy, and Josh—and the force of evil—aka You-Know-Who.

"Are you going to finish that?"

I snapped out of my daze to find Ned leaning over from his log. He was staring at my half-eaten bowl of papaya-and-rice porridge, which had been sitting forgotten on my lap for the past five minutes.

"I guess not." I handed it to him. "Here, it's all yours."

"Thanks." Ned started spooning down the porridge hungrily. "Hey, you guys," he said to the group at large with his mouth full. "What are we having for dinner at the beach-party thing tomorrow?"

"Don't worry," Ryan bragged. "You won't be disappointed. It's totally going to be awesome."

"Oh, yeah?" Brooke said with a grin. "Not half as awesome as our decorations! We spent all afternoon making garlands, and tomorrow we're going to—"

Angela looked up from her food with a frown. "Hey," she interrupted. "I don't think we should talk about the dance right now."

Weather's Here, Wish You Were Great

"Why not?" Brooke demanded. Brooke doesn't like to be interrupted.

Angela shrugged. "It's supposed to be something different and special, you know?" she said. "I just think it'll be more fun if we keep, you know, an element of mystery about it."

Glancing around at the others' fire-lit faces, I could see that I wasn't the only one who was a little skeptical about that. Personally I suspected Angela was worried that the rest of us would find out we were all working a lot harder than she was to get ready for the dance. Not that anyone with at least one working eye didn't know that already.

Brooke shrugged. "Whatever," she said. "What do you want to talk about, then? It's not like we can discuss last night's TV shows or how we did on our latest math quiz."

Ryan snorted with laughter, sending a few half-chewed chunks of papaya flying out of his mouth. "Yeah," he added. "Or what we're doing this coming weekend."

"I know what *I'm* hoping to be doing this coming weekend," Chrissie spoke up. "Getting rescued! Or even better—sitting at home being thankful that we got rescued already."

Brooke smiled. "Yeah, me too. I'm thinking Ms. Watson is going to come chugging in on some luxury liner, say, the day after tomorrow. There will be a bunch of showers on board, and an all-you-can-eat buffet with every type of food in the world."

"And a hot tub," Cassie called out. "So we can relax and recover from our ordeal."

"And watch TV," Ned added eagerly.

Josh grinned. "After all this, we'll probably be *on* TV."

Ryan shook his head. "Forget the luxury cruise ship, guys," he said. "That's much too boring. I think Ms. Watson is going to come get us on a submarine instead."

"Or a spaceship!" Kenny exclaimed. "Like the one Dani took to Earth from her home planet."

"How about a hot-air balloon?" Chrissie cried. "That would explain why it's taking her so long to get here."

"Yeah," Cassie said with a giggle. "Either that, or her boat ran out of gas and she's being towed here by dolphins."

"More like sea turtles," I joked.

Macy had been keeping pretty quiet, as usual. But just then she looked up from her bowl of food. "Why do you think it's taking so long for them to find us, anyway?"

Her soft voice cut through the silly mood like a knife,

deflating us all like a bunch of popped balloons. Nobody said anything for a second. We all just looked at one another.

Finally Josh shrugged. "I don't know," he said. "I mean, it's only been, like, five days, which isn't really that long. But I still thought someone would be here by now."

"Me too," Brooke admitted.

Chrissie bit her lip, her brown eyes wide and worried. "Me three," she added. "And it's totally freaking me out. If they haven't found us by now, who knows how long it might take them."

"I just hope my parents aren't too worried," Ryan put in, sounding more subdued than I'd ever heard him. "I'm their only kid, you know?"

Suddenly Angela jumped to her feet. "Hey," she said abruptly. "I changed my mind. I can't stand not talking about the beach dance for another second. See, it's going to be so cool, because my General Planning Committee spent, like, an hour smoothing out a place on the beach for a dance floor, and we came up with a bunch of ideas for fun dance steps everyone could try, like from videos and stuff, and . . ."

I stared at her as she babbled on and on, surprised to

find a brief, tiny sliver of respect—or at least, lack of total loathing—flickering in my heart. Even if Angela's motives were completely evil and selfish, the beach dance wasn't turning out to be such a terrible idea after all. It was giving us all something to look forward to, something to take our minds off our situation. We might not know when we were going home, but we knew the party would take place the following night. And that was something.

I guess everyone else was feeling sort of the same way, because we all started chattering eagerly about our preparations and plans for the dance. We discussed what we'd done that day, then traded ideas about other stuff we could do tomorrow.

"You know, there's just one problem," Brooke commented after a while. "We still don't have a name for the dance—or the island. Every uncharted desert isle needs a name, right? You know, like Treasure Island, Blackbeard's Island, Gilligan's Island—"

Ned gasped. "Hey, that's it!" he exclaimed. "I know the perfect name for this place!"

I rolled my eyes. "Sorry, but I think Gilligan's Island is already taken."

"No, not that." He shook his head, his blue eyes gleam-

ing in the glow from the fire. "But thinking about the show just gave me the idea."

He started humming the theme song from *Gilligan's Island.* The rest of us kept quiet and stared at one another, wondering if someone had slipped a little choo-choo bug into his porridge.

When he neared the end of the song, Ned switched from humming to singing. "... seven stranded castaways," he croaked out off-key. Then he stopped singing and grinned at us. "That's it, get it?" he said. "Castaways. That's what we are. We could call this place Castaway Island!"

There was a moment of silence as we all took that in. Then, one by one, we started to smile.

"Castaway Island!" Cassie cried. "That's perfect!"

For once, we were all in agreement. And that's how Castaway Island got its name.

Six

The moment I stepped away from the shade of the shelter the next morning, the heat slapped me in the face like a steaming rag. It was shaping up to be the hottest day yet on the island, and that was really saying something. The sun's rays beat down mercilessly, except when a few chunks of grumpy-looking grayish clouds occasionally floated by, and there wasn't the slightest hint of a breeze.

But we didn't have time to complain about the weather. We had too much to do. While the Food Committee huddled over the fire and the prep table and made occa-

sional dashes into the jungle for more ingredients, the three of us on the Decorations Committee went into a frenzy of vine weaving, flower picking, and shell gathering. I don't know what Angela's group was doing, but they spent a lot of time rushing around looking busy, so I guess they were working pretty hard too.

Despite the stultifying heat, most of the day flew by. My team and I were at the edge of the jungle decorating the "dance floor" the others had created there when I looked up and noticed the sun was already way more than halfway across the sky. What I could see of it, anyway. The clouds had built up since that morning and were crowding one another as they scudded along overhead, while a brisk, rather gusty wind sent dead leaves swirling over the beach like circling seagulls.

"Great," Brooke panted as she struggled to keep our largest vine garland from blowing off into the wild blue yonder. "*Now* there's a breeze."

"Breeze?" Ned said. "More like a gust." He glanced worriedly toward the sky. "It looks pretty cloudy. I hope it's not going to storm."

"Maybe it'll rain a little bit to cool things off," I said as I secured one end of the vine to a tree trunk with a bit

of rope. "I'm sure it'll clear up by dinnertime like usual, though. Come on, let's finish getting these things up, just in case it starts to drizzle or whatever."

The closer it got to zero hour, the more my stomach seemed to be trying to twist itself into a pretzel. How was I going to pull this off? I kept having terrible visions of how the evening might go—I could almost picture myself standing around on the sidelines with a fake smile pasted on my face, trying not to stare as Angela and Josh danced the night away. I was starting to wish I'd never come up with Operation DJ. Better yet, I wished I'd faked mono or bubonic plague or something so my parents would have let me stay home from the whole stupid trip. Why do all the best ideas always pop into your head when it's way too late?

We were just hanging the last garland when the twins appeared, looking eager and excited. "Come on, Dani," they urged. "It's time to start getting ready!"

Brooke glanced at her watch with a worried expression. "Yeah, I need to get dressed too," she said. "But we still have to finish making the flower arch, and we haven't put up the torches yet—"

"Don't worry about it," Ned said. "I can do that stuff.

It'll only take me a few minutes to change clothes."

I was a little surprised Ned was even planning to change. As far as I could recall, he'd been wearing the same khaki shorts and black flip-flops since the shipwreck. But Brooke and I nodded gratefully and took off, Brooke heading toward the supply cave where most of our luggage was stored, while the twins dragged me off in the opposite direction.

"Hey, wait," I protested. "I need to get my clothes and stuff."

"Already taken care of," Chrissie replied briskly, not slowing her pace.

Cassie glanced at me and nodded sympathetically. "We looked through your bags, but you didn't really have anything appropriate for tonight. So we've been putting together an outfit for you."

That sounded a little ominous. But I kept quiet and followed them into the jungle.

We emerged into a small clearing along the stream. Macy was already there, sitting on a large rock surrounded by suitcases, backpacks, and duffel bags.

"Hey, you changed already!" Chrissie exclaimed when she saw her.

Macy nodded and glanced shyly down at herself. She was dressed in a knee-length flowered sundress. I wasn't sure why she'd decided to bring an outfit like that along on a trash cleanup trip, but I had to admit she looked nice.

Cassie tilted her head thoughtfully. "You know, Macy, you'd look really pretty with a little makeup, maybe some lip gloss and a touch of eyeliner. And I'm sure I could do your hair up into a really awesome French braid . . ."

"Later," Chrissie told her twin shortly. "We've got to deal with Dani first."

That definitely sounded ominous. "Okay," I said briskly, deciding to take charge before they turned me into some kind of My Little Pony makeover toy. "I was thinking I could wear my light-blue shorts—those are still pretty clean. And maybe a white T-shirt—" I cut myself off when I noticed the horrified looks on their faces. "What?"

"You can't wear shorts and a T-shirt to a dance!" Cassie's tone indicated that such a thing was, in her mind, roughly equivalent to appearing at school naked.

I frowned. "So what am I supposed to wear? I forgot to pack my ball gown and high heels."

"Don't worry. Like we were saying, we've got you covered. Cass, want to grab her clothes?" Chrissie looked me

up and down with a critical eye while her sister scurried over and started digging through one of the bags. "You'd better get dressed before we do your hair and makeup. That way you won't smudge anything."

"Ta-da!" Cassie returned clutching several items of clothing. First she held up a pair of silky black shorts. "These are Chrissie's, but she wants you to wear them. And this is mine." She pulled out a scrap of bright-blue-and-white spandex that I immediately recognized as the top half of her favorite tankini.

"You want me to wear *that*?" I could almost picture Angela's amused smirk and the others' horrified stares already. "Why don't you just have me go out there in my underwear?"

Cassie held up the last item, a semisheer, short-sleeved white blouse with lacy hems. "Don't panic. You can put this over it," she said. "If you tie it at the waist, it'll look really classy and dressy."

I shot an indecisive glance at Macy. She shrugged. "I think it could look nice," she offered. "You could at least try it on, right?"

"I suppose." I sighed loudly as I grabbed the clothes from Cassie. "But no laughing, okay?"

I ducked behind a handy shrub on the stream bank to change, quickly splashing most of the caked-on sweat and dirt off myself in the clear, cool water before pulling on the twins' clothes. The tankini top exposed way more of my belly button than was normally visible anywhere outside my own shower. But the shorts fit pretty well, billowing out around my legs almost like a skirt, and once I slipped on the white shirt, I felt pretty good about the whole outfit.

Taking a deep breath—as deep as the spandex around my ribs would allow, anyway—I stepped out and twirled around. "Ta-da!" I said. "How's this?"

Cassie clapped her hands. "Yay!" she cried as she jumped forward to expertly tie the edges of the shirt together a few inches above the waist of the shorts. "You look adorable, Dani! Josh is hardly going to recognize you."

I wasn't sure that was really much of a compliment, but I figured she meant well. "Thanks," I said, shooting a slightly troubled glance down at my belly button, which was showing again. Oh, well—I figured it would be dark by party time.

"Okay," Chrissie said with a satisfied smile. "Now let's do your face. Where's your makeup bag?"

Weather's Here, Wish You Were Great

I stared at her blankly. "My what?"

I guess it was inconceivable to the twins that all I'd brought along in the way of cosmetics was a tube of Chap Stick and some sunscreen. It took me about five minutes to convince them it was true.

When it finally sank in, the two of them held a hurried, worried conference over on the stream bank before returning to stare at me. "Look," Cassie said, chewing her lower lip nervously. "Most of our makeup won't really work on you—your skin tone is way different from ours."

"Sorry I forgot to pack the entire Mary Kay White Girl Collection for this trip along with my work gloves and bug spray," I said. "Guess I'll have to go with the natural look."

Chrissie glanced over at Macy. "I don't suppose you have any makeup with you."

It was more of a statement than a question, but Macy shook her head. "My parents don't let me wear makeup."

Cassie's jaw dropped in horror, but Chrissie was already tapping her chin with her finger, thinking hard. "Brooke probably has some stuff, but her skin's even darker than ours," she murmured, more to herself than to us. "And, of course, the guys won't have anything we can use. . . ."

"The only girl whose skin tone is close to Dani's is Angela," Cassie pointed out.

I shuddered. This night was shaping up to be humiliating enough without begging the Evil One for a few extra drops of "Flirty Fuchsia" face powder.

"No way," I said. "Nothing that touches her prissy little face is coming anywhere near mine. I'd rather squeeze the insides out of a choo-choo bug and use that for lip gloss."

"You're right," Chrissie said reluctantly, though thankfully she wasn't referring to my choo-choo bug idea. "We can't ask Angela. It might give away our plans." She sighed. "Oh, well, I guess we'll just have to make do with our stuff."

They dragged out a makeup kit that would have put an average department store cosmetics counter to shame. Even Macy looked impressed as they pulled out bottle after tube after vial of various potions and concoctions. They spent the next ten or fifteen minutes experimenting on my face, like toddlers playing with finger paints. The first lip gloss they tried gave me a weird sort of death-by-drowning appearance, and even the lightest shade of blush they had made me resemble Bozo the Clown. By the time they finished dabbing things on and rubbing them off

again, my skin felt like sandpaper and my patience was wearing thin. Macy watched the whole production silently, looking by turns bored, amused, and alarmed.

Finally the twins arrived at a result that seemed to satisfy them. "There," Chrissie said, stepping back and looking me over. "That's pretty good."

"Want to see?" Cassie handed me a mirrored compact.

I peered at my face in the tiny mirror. My eyes looked strange and grown up staring back at me from within several layers of liner, shadow, and mascara, and a coating of tinted lip gloss made my mouth seem fuller than it really was. Even my sunburn looked a little less lobstery than usual, though the powder they'd used gave me a weirdly bronzy sort of sheen.

"I don't know," I said dubiously. "I don't really look like myself."

"Sure you do," Chrissie said. "Only better. Now, what should we do with your hair?"

Fortunately that part went a little more smoothly. We all agreed that my longish red hair would look best pulled back and pinned on top of my head. Luckily the twins had a large collection of barrettes, hair bands, and bobby pins in their bags.

"Cute," I declared when they finished their work, once again checking myself out in the mirror. "If I do say so myself."

"Totally cute," Cassie agreed. "Hold still."

She stepped toward me, holding a waxy white jungle flower she'd just plucked from a nearby bush. Before I could stop her, she tucked it behind my left ear.

"Ew," I said, reaching for it. "Cheesy much?"

Chrissie smacked my hand before I could grab the flower. "Leave it!" she insisted sternly. "You look great. See?"

Once again I looked in the mirror. In my opinion the flower made me look way too much like one of those swoony heroines from the cover of a trashy romance novel. But what did I know? The twins were beaming at me like doting grandparents, and they probably knew better than I did what looked good. At least I hoped so.

"Are you sure it doesn't look too stupid?" I asked uncertainly, turning the mirror this way and that to get all the different angles.

"You look gorgeous," Chrissie said as Cassie nodded vigorously.

Still not quite ready to trust them, I glanced at Macy.

"What do you think?" I asked her. "Thumbs up or thumbs down on the flower?"

Macy smiled and shot me a double thumbs-up. The exchange seemed to remind the twins of the other girl's existence.

"Okay, Macy," Chrissie said. "Your turn . . ."

I had to grin at Macy's expression of alarm. Before she knew what hit her, the twins descended with their hair-brush and makeup kit. When they stepped back ten minutes later, Macy looked a little shell-shocked but also surprisingly pretty. The twins' light touch with their makeup brushes had brought out Macy's small, even features and expressive eyes. Even her overlong, under-conditioned hair looked nice wrapped around her head in a perfect French braid.

"Wow," Macy said uncertainly when the twins handed her the mirror.

Just then Cassie glanced at her watch and let out a squeak of alarm. "It's almost seven o'clock!" she cried. "We only have, like, half an hour to finish getting ready!"

The twins raced around like the Two Stooges, bumping into each other and bouncing off of trees as they scrambled to get themselves dressed and made up. I sat

down on a suitcase near Macy and watched, resisting the almost constant urge to rub my eyes, yank at the hem of my tankini top, or pull the flower out of my hair.

After a surprisingly brief argument over who got to wear which outfit, Chrissie ended up in a purple shorts set, while Cassie pulled on a denim sundress with thin spaghetti straps.

"How do I look?" Cassie twisted and turned, trying to see herself in the tiny makeup mirror. "Does this dress look okay, or should I wear the green shorts outfit?"

I didn't have the heart to tell her that her numerous mosquito and choo-choo bites made her back look like a map of the Milky Way. Instead I smiled weakly. "Looks great."

Chrissie finished tying back her thick black hair and hurried over to sit down beside me. "Okay, listen up, Dani," she said. "We need to talk about proper party flirting behavior."

"Yeah," Cassie put in. "You're going to have to really turn on the charm tonight."

I reached up and pretended to adjust my nose like a dial. "There," I said. "Charm switched on."

"A sense of humor. That's great." Chrissie patted my

knee. "But it's going to take more than that if you want to beat Angela at her own game."

Cassie nodded. "Just remember, the main thing is to make Josh feel appreciated and important," she said. "Guys love that. Laugh at his jokes—"

"But not too hard," Chrissie warned. "You don't want to sound like a giggly airhead. Try to talk about stuff he's interested in."

"But talk about stuff you like sometimes too," Cassie put in. "That way he'll know you're your own person. And try to touch him whenever you can—you know, like pat him on the hand, let your shoulder brush against his, that kind of thing."

I felt my face go pink under my makeup as I recalled clocking Josh on the shoulder the afternoon before. Somehow I didn't think that was quite what Cassie had in mind.

They went on for a while with more helpful hints, but I kind of stopped listening. I seriously doubted I would be able to follow any of their advice with a straight face. Even if I managed it, it would probably just confirm Josh's suspicion that I'd swallowed a choo-choo bug in my sleep and gone as wacko as Mr. Truskey.

"Hello, girls." Angela's snotty voice interrupted my thoughts as well as the twins' comments. She stepped into the clearing holding a water jug and looking fresh and flawless in a white tank top, blue miniskirt, and white leather sandals. "It's almost time for the beach dance to start, you know. Don't be late!"

I scowled at her, wondering if she'd overheard any of our conversation. But she barely spared me a second, albeit slightly surprised, glance as she quickly scooped some water out of the stream and then disappeared again.

"Wow," Cassie whispered when the Evil One was gone. "She looks great tonight, doesn't she?"

"Yeah." Chrissie stared at me for a moment, her dark eyes worried. Then she shrugged. "That's okay," she said. "Dani has her beat all the way on personality."

That didn't exactly make me feel better. Neither did Cassie's next words.

"Good point," she said. "Besides, we already know Josh has the hots for Dani. All she has to do is let him know she likes him back, then reel him in."

"Hold on," I protested, my stomach flip-flopping nervously. "Let's not get carried away with that stuff. I don't like him that way, remember? And I definitely don't

want to, like, lead him on by begging to be his girlfriend or something."

The twins didn't respond, merely trading amused glances. Even Macy looked a little skeptical.

I clenched my fists at my sides, irritation welling up and churning around in my gut along with the nervousness, until I thought I might barf. All I wanted to do was save a nice guy from Evil Angela's clutches. Why couldn't anyone understand that?

At that moment there was a crashing sound from the jungle nearby. I think we were all expecting to see Angela reappear. Instead Kenny burst into the clearing, red faced and wide eyed.

"Dani!" he blurted out. "There you are!"

"What are you doing here, you nose-picking little troll?" I exclaimed, startled by his sudden appearance. "Get lost. This is a girls-only clearing—so shoo!"

He hardly seemed to hear me. "You've got to come look at my zoo," he cried.

I frowned slightly, noticing that he looked really upset. Figuring that one of his beetles had probably just been chomped by one of his toads or something, I decided to try to be nice. "Sorry, twerp," I said as patiently as I could

manage. "Bad timing. You're not going to have much luck luring people to your bug circus tonight of all nights."

"Huh?" Kenny stared at me blankly.

"The beach party," I said. "Tonight. Remember?"

His eyes lit up briefly. "Oh, yeah!" he said, licking his lips. "That's when we're having the big special dinner, right?"

"Right." Cassie checked her watch. "And we've got to get down there right now before the others eat everything without us."

Kenny stared at her, the anxious expression returning to his face. "Wait!" he cried. "First you guys have to come check out my zoo. The animals are acting weird. Like, all upset and hyper and stuff, even the ones that usually sleep most of the time."

"Sorry, Kenny," Macy said kindly. "Maybe we'll all go take a look tomorrow, okay?"

"No, now!" Kenny insisted, his voice rising to a squeaky sort of screech. "I think something's wrong with them!"

"Of course something's wrong with them," I retorted, losing whatever sympathy for him I'd mustered before. I wasn't in the mood for his antics. "They're trapped in your dorky little zoo. How do you expect them to act?" I glanced at the other girls. "Come on, you guys, let's get out of here."

Weather's Here, Wish You Were Great

Yelling at my little brother actually helped me feel a bit more normal. As the four of us left both the clearing and Kenny behind and headed out to the beach, I was almost calm.

Chrissie shot me a sidelong glance as we neared the edge of the woods. "Ready for this?" she murmured.

I nodded, doing my best to psyche myself up for the coming ordeal. "Ready as I'll ever be," I replied. "I'll try not to let you guys down."

Cassie smiled. "Operation DJ forever!" she whispered.

Then we all stepped out onto the beach, and for a moment I forgot all about everything else as I looked around in amazement. The place had been completely transformed by all our hard work. The sun was setting, but there was still plenty of light by which to admire the garlands of vines, the flowers everywhere, the stones and torches and palm fronds. It was still kind of windy, but somehow that made everything look even cooler—like the island itself was already dancing.

Ryan and Josh were standing proudly near the fire pit, which looked a lot fancier than usual thanks to the pretty shells and sparkly stones we had added to the ring of rocks surrounding it. The Food Committee had dragged

the food-prep table over to the edge of the dance floor and dressed it up with a "tablecloth" of palm fronds and a centerpiece of fresh tropical flowers stuck into a big conch shell. Six places were set on the table; the few dishes we'd salvaged from our boat were supplemented with ones made from coconut shells, flat stones, empty food containers, and seashells. Large tropical leaves served as napkins, and someone had pulled apart our life-preserver mattress to create slightly tattered life-preserver cushions as seating. Five more places were set on a bare, rocky shelf at the base of the cliff nearby. The other castaways were standing in a little cluster at the edge of the beach. Even Mr. Truskey was there, along with Kenny, who had arrived just behind us, still looking rather upset.

"Wow," Cassie exclaimed, taking it all in. "Check this place out!"

Chrissie nodded, shielding her face with one hand as a gust blew a few leaves past us. "It looks amazing! Even the sunset looks extra special tonight."

I glanced up. Rays of red, orange, pink, and every possible shade of gold were smeared across the entire sky, and rosy light glistened off the sand and shells and

made the faces of my schoolmates look mysterious and unfamiliar.

Just then I noticed Josh glancing our way. I gulped, some of my anxiety creeping back. "Come on," I said. "Looks like everyone else is already here."

We hurried to join the others. "Greetings, people!" Mr. Truskey cried at our arrival, raising one hand in greeting. I noticed he had a leaf tied around his neck, which I guessed was supposed to be a bow tie. "Welcome to Fantasy Island. May I take your coats?"

"No thanks, Mr. T." With difficulty I choked back a giggle. I felt bad for wanting to laugh—after all, it wasn't his fault he was crazy.

But there's just something about being all dressed up and anticipating something out of the ordinary that seems to make everyone jittery—quick to laugh and maybe a little clumsy. Ryan and Ned started clowning around, shoving and trying to trip each other. Brooke was chattering excitedly at Josh, her words pouring out so fast it was impossible to figure out what she was saying. I swallowed hard a few times, wondering why my throat suddenly felt as dry as if I'd just gulped down half the sand on the beach.

Castaways

Only Angela appeared unaffected by the giddy mood. Looking as cool as a cocky little cucumber, she swished forward in her blue miniskirt and called for attention.

"Good evening, everyone," she said loudly, sounding self-important and rather melodramatic. "I'd like to officially welcome everyone to the First Annual Castaway Island Beach Dance."

"I hope it's also the *Last* Annual Castaway Island Beach Dance," Ryan called out.

Everyone laughed at that, even Angela. Ryan grinned, then let out an enthusiastic whoop.

"Come on!" he shouted, pumping his fist in the air. "Let the beach party begin!"

Seven

"Good thing I brought extra batteries," Ned commented as he switched on his radio, which for some reason made everyone laugh again.

The radio burst into staticky life and fast-paced salsa music poured out of the tiny speakers. It wasn't exactly the sound system at Radio City Music Hall, but it sounded pretty good after going so long with no music at all.

"Should we eat first?" Ned peered in the direction of the fire pit. "We don't want the food to get cold."

For the first time I noticed a tantalizing scent mixing with the everyday odors of sea and jungle. Food. Actual

cooked food. I followed Ned's gaze and saw a variety of pots and pans bubbling over the flames.

"Sounds good to me," I said hungrily.

Josh, Chrissie, and Ryan led the way toward the dining area. "Party of, er, eleven, your table is ready," Ryan announced with a deep, swooping bow. "Please seat yourselves."

"Hurry up," Cassie hissed into my ear, grabbing my arm and hustling me forward. "Make sure you get a seat next to you-know-who."

There was a moment of chaos as everyone dashed for the tables. Josh took the middle spot on one side of the door-table, and I headed for the seat on his left. But I was a little too slow—Mr. Truskey lurched out of nowhere, flopping down on the life-preserver cushion and grabbing his leaf napkin.

"Waiter! Oh, waiter! I'm ready to see the wine list," he declared, looking deranged but happy.

Out of the corner of my eye I saw Angela dart forward toward the spot on Josh's right. Before she could get there, Cassie stepped forward, bumping into Angela and spinning her off track.

"Oops," Cassie said sweetly. "Sorry about that."

Weather's Here, Wish You Were Great

By the time Angela turned around, Kenny had plopped himself down in the empty spot beside Josh. I grinned. At least my little brother had come in handy for once. I contemplated forcing him to give me his seat, but I didn't want to be too obvious.

Brooke was already sitting directly across from Josh, so I had to settle for the seat to her left. Cassie dashed around the table, snagging the last seat before Angela could get there.

Seeing that she was shut out, Angela scowled. I smiled sweetly at her. "Guess you'll have to sit over there," I said, waving a hand toward the rock ledge.

She glared at me, then stalked off without a word.

That was probably the most delicious part of the whole dinner. But the food was great too. The three chefs had outdone themselves, concocting a sort of seafood medley casserole by combining our last few boxes of crackers with the mussels, crabs, and clams they'd collected. There was also a salad of greens and shoots, a tasty soup made out of leftover canned food from the boat, and a coconut-and-papaya dessert. Passing the dishes around again and again as the setting sun's dramatic rays faded into darkness, we all ate until we squeaked.

Castaways

Unfortunately it all went downhill from there. I was holding my stomach and wondering if I could manage one more helping of dessert when I saw Angela hop up from her spot and hurry over to our table. "I love this song," she simpered, batting her eyes at Josh. "So how about that dance you promised me?"

Seeing Cassie's surprised look, I realized I'd forgotten to tell my coconspirators that Josh had already promised Angela the first dance. To tell the truth, I think I'd sort of blocked it out of my mind. It all came rushing back as Josh dabbed at his lips with his napkin and stood up, looking slightly sheepish.

"Excuse me," he mumbled vaguely at the rest of us. "Um, why don't you all come on out and dance too?"

I gritted my teeth as Angela took him by the arm and dragged him toward the dance floor. The salsa song playing at the moment had a slow, lazy, ballady sort of beat.

"Favorite song, my butt," I mumbled under my breath, certain that Angela had never heard it before in her life.

Brooke glanced over at me. "What?" she asked with her mouth full of coconut.

"Nothing," I muttered, still staring intently toward the dance floor.

Weather's Here, Wish You Were Great

When Josh and Angela turned to face each other, he put his hands out, fumbling awkwardly at her waist. She ignored that, stepping forward and wrapping her arms around his neck as if she was holding on to keep from drowning. It was too dark to see the expression on his face, though I imagined hopefully that it might involve something like loathing. Or disgust. Or at the very least, extreme embarrassment. He held his hands out in the air for a second or two before resting them gingerly on her back.

"You heard what Josh said," Ryan called out, leaping to his feet. "We should all get out there and boogie! Come on, Dani—you look like you've got boogie fever!"

He leaped over and grabbed my hand, dragging me to my feet. "Ugh," I groaned. "Oh, all right." Maybe getting out on the dance floor would give me a better view of Josh's expression. I just hoped Ryan didn't expect me to hang all over him like Angela was doing to Josh. Because that? Not happening.

Fortunately Ryan didn't seem interested in Angela's type of slow-dancing and instead started gyrating wildly while clutching one of my hands tightly in his own, paying absolutely no attention whatsoever to the actual beat

of the song. I shuffled my feet around in the sand, glaring over at Angela. She didn't notice. Her head was resting on Josh's shoulder and her eyes were closed. A self-satisfied smile played across her face.

However, now that I was closer I could see that Josh was standing stiffly, his eyes wide open. He looked decidedly uncomfortable with the whole situation, though he made no move to peel Angela off him or anything.

Finally the slow song ended, and an up-tempo number took its place. Angela loosened her grip and allowed Josh to escape. He backed away, looking relieved. Or was that my imagination? The dim, flickering light from the torches and lanterns made it difficult to tell for sure. I wished the moon would hurry up and come out already, but when I glanced up, there wasn't a hint of it. Even the stars, usually as bright as tiny car headlights, were hidden behind a thick layer of clouds.

Most of the others had joined us on the dance floor by now, though Kenny was still sitting over by the food and Mr. Truskey had wandered off. The rest of us danced in a big, shifting group for the next twenty or thirty minutes. First I would find myself swaying beside the twins or Macy, then matching wild steps with Ryan or doing a

sort of slow groove along with Ned. The radio station was pretty staticky, and the spirited salsa wasn't exactly the type of music we were accustomed to at school dances, but each person seemed to have his or her own unique interpretation of it—some more creative than others. Once I stopped glaring at Angela and let myself get into the mood of the night, I actually started having fun. It was nice to forget about everything—getting rescued, Mr. Truskey's mental health, Angela's evilness—and just dance.

After a while I ducked out of the dancing mob and hurried over to grab a drink from the water jug on the table. As soon as I stopped moving I noticed that the breeze had picked up even more since dinner, turning into a stiff, cool wind whipping in off the water. In seconds the sweat had evaporated from my face and body, and I was shivering.

"It's getting kind of cold, isn't it?" a voice spoke out of the darkness.

I jumped, realizing that Kenny was sitting there just a few feet away. The campfire had died down some, though the flames that were left were flickering wildly and spitting sparks into the wind.

Castaways

"What are you doing sitting there like that?" I demanded. "You scared me half to death."

Kenny shrugged. "I'm just watching you guys dance."

I stared at him. A brief, passing touch of pity sneaked its way through me. Kenny looked really young and sort of out of place sitting there alone. It had to be hard being the only little kid stranded with a bunch of middle-schoolers.

Just then Macy appeared at my side. "Is there any water left?" she asked breathlessly. Her cheeks were pink with exertion, making her look really pretty.

I handed her the jug, happy to see that she seemed to be having fun. Had she ever attended one of the school dances back at Tweedale? I had no idea.

After she drank, she smiled at Kenny. "Hey, Ken," she said. "You don't have to sit over here all alone. Why don't you come dance?"

Kenny looked uncertain. He shot me a quick glance. "I dunno . . . ," he mumbled.

Macy laughed and grabbed his hand. "Come on," she urged playfully. "You're not supposed to say no when a lady asks you to dance, you know. It's not polite."

"A lady?" Kenny giggled. "I don't see any ladies around here."

"Why, you . . ." Pretending to growl with anger, Macy leaned in to tickle him.

I wrinkled my nose as he shrieked with delight and raced toward the dance floor with Macy right behind him. A second later he was flinging himself all over the place like a frog having seizures.

"Lovely," I muttered to myself. "Like just being related to him isn't embarrassing enough . . ."

As I wandered back toward the dance floor I saw Josh break away from the group, step out past the torches, and come toward me. For a second I thought he was just going over for a drink, but he stopped in front of me. "Having fun?" he asked.

The nearest torch was directly behind him, casting his face into deep shadow and making it impossible to read his expression. I gulped as all the twins' advice suddenly crowded into my head. For a second I was ready to try again—to attempt once more to flirt as they had taught me.

Smile, I told myself. Act interested in him. Laugh at his jokes. Ask him questions about himself. . . .

But even as I opened my mouth to try, I knew I couldn't do it. No way. It just wasn't me. Besides, I respected Josh

too much as a person to act fake with him. He deserved better than that—and so did I. If that meant Angela and her more obvious wiles might win his heart, so be it. At least I would still be able to live with myself.

I smiled, proud of my own sudden burst of wisdom. Realizing that Josh was staring at me uncertainly, obviously wondering why it was taking me, like, half an hour to answer a simple question, I gulped and then smiled.

"Yeah," I told him. "I wasn't too sure about this whole beach-party idea at first. But I'm glad we decided to do it." I swallowed back the next few words: *Even if it was Angela's idea.*

Josh returned my smile. "Me too."

Just then the music on the radio changed again. Another slow song started to play.

I held my breath, staring at Josh and wondering what to do or say next.

"Hey," Josh said, his voice so quiet I had to lean forward a little to hear it. "Do you, um, you know—do you want to dance?"

Eight

"Do I—wha . . . erk, um, ulp . . ."
I stammered for a moment or two with great eloquence, not sure whether I'd heard him right. Then I swallowed hard, hoping he couldn't hear my heart as it tried to hammer its way out of my chest in shock. "Er, what?"

"Dance?" Josh sounded slightly worried. "Um, I mean, if you want to . . ."

"Yes!" I blurted out. "Uh, I mean, that sounds good. Sure. Okay." I nodded a few times just to make the point clear.

"Good," Josh said, sounding relieved. "Um, come on."

We walked together toward the dance floor. I felt weird

111

and sort of light-headed, and my limbs seemed very heavy and slow, as if I was trying to walk through Vaseline. Even so, I was vaguely aware that Angela was charging toward us, probably hoping to bully Josh into another slow dance.

I don't know if Josh saw her. If so, he gave no sign of it. Instead he turned toward me and placed both his hands gently on my waist. It felt so weird that for a second I just stood there, a little panicky as I wondered what I was supposed to do. I'd never slow-danced with a boy before. Not that I'm making excuses, by the way—I admit it was a huge dorkozoid brain freeze moment. I might not be *el girly-girl supremo* like Angela, who probably spent every spare moment dreaming of stuff like her first real dance, but I wasn't completely clueless either. It was just that when the moment arrived, I got a little nervous and sort of blanked out on the exact procedure.

Luckily the twins came to my rescue. I guess they were keeping a close eye on me and figured out what was happening. They raced over and stood behind Josh, so he couldn't see them but I could. Then Chrissie planted her hands on Cassie's waist, just as Josh had

done with me. Next Cassie gracefully draped her arms over her twin's shoulders.

My eyes lit up. "Oh, yeah!" I blurted out.

Josh blinked. "Excuse me?"

"Nothing." I quickly arranged my hands just as Cassie had done, hoping the dim light hid my red face. Josh's short-sleeved button-down felt soft and sort of rustly under my hands, and I could feel the warmth of his skin through the thin fabric.

"Um, that flower looks nice," Josh said shyly.

"What?" I glanced around, wondering which flower he meant. There were blossoms everywhere—woven into the garlands, drifted over rocks, tied to the torches. They were a big part of our decorating scheme.

Suddenly I remembered the flower tucked into my hair. I blushed, realizing that was probably what he meant. Oops.

"Uh, I mean, thanks," I said hastily.

He looked slightly confused, but he smiled. "You're welcome."

I held my breath as we started to dance. Well, it was more like we started swaying carefully from side to side

as we rotated slowly in a circle. But technically, it was dancing. And I think I sort of almost maybe liked it. A little. I mean, I wasn't sure where to look, and I couldn't help feeling a little awkward. Our arms were almost straight out from our bodies—I think we were both being careful not to stand too close. It certainly wasn't the way Angela had done it. . . .

That reminded me to wonder whether the Evil One was watching. I started to glance around for her, hoping to see her spontaneously combusting from sheer rage and jealousy. As I turned my head something splatted into my left eye, half blinding me for a second.

"Hey," I cried, blinking furiously. I glanced up—just in time to feel another huge splat right in the middle of my forehead.

I felt Josh's grip on my waist loosening. He rubbed at his own face. "Yo, I think it's raining," he said.

Talk about bad timing! Even as it started to drizzle in earnest, I was ready to tough it out and keep dancing. But as a general hue and cry went up from the others, Josh dropped his hands and took a few steps back. Bummer!

Within seconds the drizzle had turned into a steady rain that doused most of the torches and made the

campfire sizzle and pop. Double bummer!

Someone grabbed the radio, and we all dashed toward the cliffs as the rain pounded down harder and harder. By the time I neared the supply cave entrance, which was almost invisible thanks to the darkness and sheeting rain, I was completely drenched—even my bones felt as if they were sloshing inside of me. I could only hope the makeup the twins had applied to my face had washed off cleanly rather than leaving me with raccoon eyes and lip-gloss chin.

I glanced up as I darted into the cave. On our very first day, we'd discovered that the caves in the cliffs that bordered part of the beach served as home base to what seemed to be the entire world's population of bats. That was why we'd opted to build a shelter on the beach rather than just using one or more of the caves. Since that time, I guess we'd all sort of gotten used to the bats, because most of us now wandered in and out of the supply cave at all hours without giving them a second thought. But that didn't mean I was thrilled at the idea of spending the night with bats flying around overhead squeaking and pooping on me.

Given the options, though, I figured I would have to live

with it. I turned and stared out at the storm. Ragged streaks of lightning were flashing out over the water in the distance, reflecting off the looming clouds just overhead and illuminating the wind-lashed waves of the lagoon.

"Wow," I said to the person beside me, whose identity was impossible to ascertain in the darkness. "It's really coming down out there."

"Way to state the obvious, genius girl," a sarcastic voice responded.

Just my luck. It was Angela.

A little farther back in the cave, a beam of light suddenly flickered to life. Josh's face was visible in the shadowy glow behind the flashlight. Its thin but steady light flickered quickly over a huddled group of wet and miserable-looking faces. I spotted Brooke and Ryan, along with several of the others.

"Is everyone here?" Josh asked.

"I'm here," I said immediately, touched by his obvious concern for the group. "Dani, that is."

"Duh," Angela muttered, squinting as Josh's flashlight passed over her face. I was pleased to see that she looked just as much like a half-drowned rat as the rest of us. "Like anyone could miss a motormouth like you."

Weather's Here, Wish You Were Great

There was a sudden burst of static. My gaze followed Josh's flashlight over to Ned, who was bent over his radio.

"Forget about the music," Brooke told him impatiently. "I think it's safe to say the first annual beach dance is over."

"Not necessarily," Chrissie spoke up. "These tropical showers usually pass pretty quickly, right?"

"Not always," her twin argued. "Remember that storm our first night here? That one lasted a while."

Ryan glanced out at the raging storm. "Yeah. Besides, I wouldn't call this a shower. More like a typhoon." He winced as a sudden gust blew a spray of cold rain into the cave entrance. "I mean, what's up with all this wind?"

I sighed, not particularly fond of it at that moment myself. Why did a stupid storm have to come along just when things were getting interesting out there on the beach? I reached up and gently touched the soggy flower still tucked into my hair.

Maybe it was for the best, though. I wasn't sure I liked the way dancing with Josh had made me feel. A shiver ran through me, from my shoulders straight down through my toes, as I remembered the soft weight of Josh's hands on my waist and the nice scent of soap wafting off him. What was wrong with me? Was I

finally succumbing to the dreaded girly-girl disease?

I shuddered again, this time with dismay. I'd seen that particular ailment strike way too many of my classmates that year. First a girl would start giggling every few minutes for no apparent reason, especially when boys were around. Then she would start reapplying lip gloss after each class and carrying around magazines containing articles with titles such as "How to Be Super Cute 'N' Stuff" or "Ten Terrific Tips for Acting Like a Ditz." Finally she would forget that there was any topic worth discussing other than boys, boys, boyzzzzz, and that would be that. She would be hopeless—another Angela clone.

But I don't do any of that stuff, I reminded myself fiercely. No way, no how. Getting a little swoony over one dance didn't mean I suddenly preferred the beauty shop to the basketball court or wanted to trade in my subscription to *Sports Illustrated* for one to *Hottie Hunks Weekly.* Did it?

I was startled out of my thoughts as another burst of static bounced off the cave walls. Ned was still crouched down nearby, fiddling with the radio dials.

"Ned!" Brooke said warningly, sounding irritated.

"Shhh," Ned said distractedly. "I'm just trying to hear . . ."

"What is it, dude?" Josh stepped closer and aimed his flashlight down onto the radio.

Ned glanced up at him, squinting worriedly into the beam. "It's getting even more staticky since this storm started."

"Major duh." Angela rolled her eyes as she tried to squeeze the water out of her hair. "That always happens during big storms. Our satellite TV goes out all the time when it rains hard."

Josh shrugged. "She's probably right," he told Ned, raising his voice a little as the static faded and salsa music pumped out clearly again. "I'm sure the reception will get better again once this—"

Beeeeep!

The song suddenly cut out, replaced by a series of loud, irritating tones. Think car alarm with an attitude.

"Ow!" Cassie squeaked, pressing her hands over her ears. "Turn that thing—"

"Quiet!" Brooke commanded, suddenly much more interested in the radio as a man's voice began speaking rapidly between beeps, fading in and out thanks to the continuing waves of static. "It sounds like some kind of news report or something. Listen!"

We all listened. The voice sounded hurried and urgent. Unfortunately I had no idea what it was saying, since it was speaking in Spanish.

I glanced over at Ryan and Josh, who speak Spanish fluently. Both of them were leaning forward over the radio, their faces squinched up in concentration as they tried to make out the words. The rest of us just held our breath—or at least, I did—and winced as each fresh burst of static drowned out the fast-talking voice.

Suddenly Ryan gasped. *"Dios mío!"* he murmured, glancing at Josh with wide, solemn eyes. "Did you hear what I think I just heard?"

Josh nodded grimly. "I think so."

"What?" Cassie demanded anxiously. "What is it? What did he say?"

"It's hard to hear for sure," Josh said slowly. "I can only make out about every other word or so, with all the static. But I think he's talking about—"

"A hurricane!" Ryan broke in. "They're saying something about a hurricane!"

Nine

"A hurricane!" Cassie shrieked. "Oh, no! We're going to die!"

"Shut up, you spaz," Chrissie cried, sounding more than a little panicky herself. "We're not going to die."

"Everyone's going to die," Ryan put in philosophically, "someday."

Brooke glared at him. "You're not helping things!" she yelled. "We have to figure out what to do!"

"Quiet!" Josh yelped desperately, waving his arms for attention. "We're trying to hear the—oops, never mind."

Castaways

We all quieted down just in time to hear the Spanish-speaking voice cut out for good, replaced by a steady stream of harsh, spitting gray static. Ned fiddled with the dials, but it was no use.

For a moment we all sat there staring at one another in the pitiful little light of the flashlight. "Now what?" Ned asked.

Brooke looked at Josh and Ryan. "Are you sure you heard them say hurricane?"

"How can they be sure?" Chrissie argued before either of the boys could answer. "You heard how staticky that was—they could have misunderstood."

"Besides, we don't know where that station was coming from. Even if they were talking about a hurricane, it doesn't mean they're necessarily talking about *this* storm." Angela waved one hand at the raging monsoon outside. "It doesn't mean a hurricane is going to hit this exact island."

I stared outside dubiously. "Come on," I said. "We're from Florida. We've all seen a hurricane or two in our time, right? What does this look like to you?"

Angela wrinkled her nose. "Way to be optimistic, Dani Doom."

Weather's Here, Wish You Were Great

"Hey, I'm just trying to be realistic here," I snapped. "You should try it someday; you might like it."

Macy bit her lip as she glanced outside. "Maybe the hurricane is just passing by offshore," she suggested tentatively. "That happens back home all the time, remember? It gets really stormy like this for a while, and that's it."

I shrugged. "Maybe," I said. "The lightning's still pretty far out to sea. So I guess that could be it."

Josh took a few steps toward the entrance. "You're right, Dani," he said. "The lightning's still far away for now. Maybe we should run out and try to clean up a little— you know, tie stuff down or whatever so it doesn't all get ruined or blown away. Just in case."

That didn't sound like a barrel of fun to me. But he had a point. While our luggage and some of our food were right there in the cave with us, a lot of our other valuable survival-type stuff—cooking pots, tarps, water jugs, lanterns—was sitting around on the beach just waiting to get blown out to sea or smashed to bits on the cliffs.

"Okay," I said, trying to sound braver than I felt. "Let's go!"

We dove out into the howling maw of the storm. Does that sound melodramatic? Good. Because that was exactly how it felt. The rain was pelting down so hard

that it was as if someone was pounding on every bit of exposed skin with a meat tenderizer. When I glanced toward the jungle during a distant flash of lightning, I could see that the trees were bent almost halfway to the ground by the wind, their tops lashing furiously around as if they were wrestling with each other.

Things were blowing around pretty good out on the beach, too. I ducked just in time to avoid getting beaned by something that might have been someone's shoe. Then again, it might have been a rock, or a seashell, or possibly a leftover can of creamed corn—it was kind of hard to tell.

A second later I jumped as something white whooshed by just inches in front of my eyes. Then I realized it was only the flower from my hair, which the wind had finally ripped away. Oh, well.

I did my best to shove everything I could find into whichever cave was closest, vaguely aware of the others running around nearby doing the same thing. As I passed the shelter at one point, I could see several flashlight beams bouncing around as a couple of people—Josh and Chrissie?—attempted to tie down one of the tarps that was flapping around wildly like some kind of giant

demented bird. I thought about stopping to help, but just then another lightning flash showed me that most of our plastic dinnerware and flatware was currently rolling or blowing across the sand toward the lagoon. Racing forward, I grabbed blindly for things, hoping I wouldn't close my fingers over an irritated crab by mistake while I tucked as many of the items as I could into my pockets or under my shirt.

Meanwhile I was careful to keep one eye on the lightning flashes out beyond the lagoon. When they seemed to be getting a little too close for comfort, I decided it was time to get inside before I became a human lightning rod.

I looked around, clutching the dishes against my stomach and blinking my eyes furiously to try to clear them of rainwater. Which way was the cave? The rain was coming down even harder now; I couldn't see more than two feet in front of my face. It was like being trapped within layer after layer of thick, impenetrable gray curtains.

Suddenly there was a massive crack of thunder that sounded as if it had erupted about three inches over my head. At the same instant the beach was bathed in a violent explosion of white-hot light as several jagged streaks

of lightning crisscrossed the sky. That was enough to give me back my bearings—and encourage me to make like a refrigerator and run.

About 2.3 seconds later I flung myself through the last curtain of rain at the entrance and sprinted into the cave. I let the dishes fall out of my shirt and then collapsed on the rough stone floor just beyond the spray zone, panting. Rolling over onto my back, I closed my eyes and waited for my adrenaline-pumped heartbeat to subside to normal.

"Wow," I said. "That was intense."

My eyelids suddenly went a weird shade of red. I opened my eyes to see Ryan peering down at me, holding one of the lanterns from the ship directly over my face. "Are you okay?" he asked.

"Yeah." I sat up, pushing a wad of waterlogged hair out of my eyes. The upswept hairdo the twins had constructed so carefully for me was long gone. "Just wet."

"Join the club," Cassie panted, flopping down beside me. "I think half my skin got washed away."

Ryan set his lantern on a ledge. It cast a thin but cheery glow over about half the cave's interior. Glancing around, I saw that Macy and Ned were huddled in the middle of the floor, while Brooke stood nearby trying to dry her-

self off with somebody's jeans. I just hoped they weren't mine. Ryan started pacing restlessly, and Cassie stared out wide-eyed at the storm, as if hypnotized by its fury.

Just then Josh dashed in from outside, followed immediately by Chrissie. "Whew!" Josh cried. "That's some storm out there. But I think we got the shelter secured—as well as we could, anyway. We'll just have to hope it holds." He looked around at the wet faces staring back at him. "Is everybody here?"

"Where's Mr. Truskey?" Ned asked.

"Uh-oh," I said. "He's probably dancing around out there, composing an ode to the hurricane tiki gods or something."

Josh looked worried. "You're right," he said. "In his condition he might not realize how dangerous it is outside. Maybe we should—"

"Kenny!" Macy cried suddenly. "He's missing too!"

My heart stopped. At least it felt that way. "Are you sure?" I demanded. "He might just be hiding back there in the dark or something, acting immature and trying to scare us." I peered into the darkness, caught halfway between worried and exasperated. "Kenny? Come on, you twerp. Quit joking around."

Castaways

There was no response. Brooke picked up a flashlight and switched it on, aiming its strong beam into the dark corners of the cave. There was no sign of Kenny, though I did hear a rather disturbing rustle from somewhere overhead.

But this was no time to be worrying about bats. Where was that bratty little brother of mine?

If I lose him, Mom and Dad will kill me, I said to myself. The weak joke fell kind of flat even inside my own head.

"He's not here," Brooke announced superfluously, still flipping the flashlight beam around the cave.

The light picked up the sudden scurry of a small lizard running for cover. As soon as I saw it, the answer flashed into my head in big, pulsing neon letters. The zoo. That had to be it. The little fool had run off to rescue his animals from the storm. It sounded exactly like something he might do.

I don't know why I didn't say anything to the others. I guess I was hoping I was wrong. Besides, they were already busy discussing other possibilities.

"Maybe he's with Mr. T," Chrissie suggested hopefully.

Brooke nodded. "They could be holed up together in one of the smaller caves."

Weather's Here, Wish You Were Great

"You're right," Josh said. "We'd better check it out." He took a deep breath, glancing out at the pelting rain, which appeared to be blowing almost directly sideways at this point. "I'll go."

"You shouldn't go out there alone," Angela protested. "It's not safe."

She had a point, though I noticed she didn't volunteer to go along herself or anything. Just as I was about to volunteer—after all, it was my brother we were looking for—Ryan jumped forward.

"I'm with you, dude," he said, clapping Josh wetly on the shoulder. "Let's hit it." Before the rest of us could say a word, they grabbed a couple of flashlights and plunged back out into the storm.

The next ten or fifteen minutes seemed to pass very, very slowly. Think frozen molasses dripping uphill. In slow motion.

Nobody said much for a while. Brooke switched off her flashlight and we all sat there staring at one another in the puddle of light from the lantern. I don't know about the others, but my mind was pretty much a blank for a while. No thoughts, no feelings, just a sort of limbo of waiting.

"Do you think they're okay out there?" Chrissie asked at last.

"I hope so," Angela said. "We probably shouldn't have let them go."

Brooke frowned. "They'll be fine. I'm sure they're just dashing from cave to cave. That means they're mostly out of the wind, so it shouldn't be too bad. They'll probably be back soon."

I noticed that none of them were looking at me. In fact, they seemed to be deliberately avoiding my gaze. That was when my brain kicked back into gear, and it really hit me. Kenny. Eight-year-old Kenny, alone somewhere on this island. In the middle of a hurricane.

Why hadn't I grabbed him on my way in, when the storm started? I knew better than anyone how irresponsible he was; I should have known something like this would happen. . . . I chewed my lower lip, not sure whether to feel more aggravated with myself or Kenny.

I settled for Angela instead. It was her stupid beach-dance idea that was to blame. If not for that, we probably would have noticed the storm rolling in a lot sooner. We would have had plenty of time to get everything tied down and put away, rather than running around like

headless chickens trying to do it in the dark, and Kenny wouldn't have been able to slip away.

I blinked my eyes rapidly, suddenly aware that I was dangerously close to tears. Maybe Kenny wasn't much of a brother, but he was the only one I had. What if I never saw him again? Alternating waves of sadness, worry, irritation, and guilt washed through me, making me feel queasy and anxious.

Just when I wasn't sure I could stand it anymore, Josh and Ryan burst into the cave with a dramatic spray of water. "Yowza!" Ryan whooped, collapsing against the dry stone of the cave wall and clinging to it as if it was a life raft. "It's getting really not-fun out there."

"Did you find them?" Macy asked anxiously.

Josh bent over, resting both hands on his knees as he huffed and puffed like all three little pigs. "We found Mr. T," he reported between gasps. "He's okay—he's snoozing away about three caves down. We just left him there."

"Kenny wasn't with him?" I asked through lips that suddenly seemed frozen with fear.

Josh straightened up, exchanged a glance with Ryan, and shook his head. "Sorry, Dani," he said quietly. "We didn't see any sign of him anywhere."

Castaways

My faint hopes crumbled and sank deep into the pit of despair that used to be my stomach. That was it, then. There was only one answer.

"Listen," I said. "I—I think I know where he might be." I quickly explained my theory about Kenny's zoo. "He's probably up there somewhere trying to rescue his stupid bugs and snakes from the storm," I finished.

"Yikes." Chrissie looked worried. "Do you really think that's where he is?"

I shrugged. "I don't know for sure. But where else would he go?"

"Yeah." Josh nodded thoughtfully. "He mentioned the zoo thing to me a few times. Seemed really psyched about it."

"Me too," Macy put in. "I'd promised to go up there with him tomorrow."

"Exactly where is this zoo?" Brooke asked.

"I'm not sure," I admitted. "Somewhere up the mountain, I guess. I've never been there—he just told me about it."

"Ditto," Josh added, and Macy shrugged.

Angela blew out a loud sigh. "Great," she muttered. "Just great."

I glared at her, but the others ignored her. "Maybe we

could make up a search party," Josh suggested uncertainly. "Go after him."

"How?" Brooke asked. "We don't even really know where to look. It's dark, it's raining, the wind is beyond crazy—we'd probably all end up blowing out to sea."

"Not if we tied ourselves together," Ryan said, though he didn't sound too excited about the idea.

Ned shook his head. "I don't know," he said. "Brooke's right. It's dangerous out there right now. Maybe if we wait an hour or so, things will let up a little and then we can try searching."

"But he's only eight!" Macy pointed out worriedly. "We can't just leave him out there."

Her words hung in the damp air for a moment. Nobody said anything, and everyone suddenly seemed very interested in examining his or her own fingers or toes. I felt as if all the air was being sucked out of my body as I realized the truth: Everybody was reluctant to admit that they didn't want to go back out in the storm to search for my brother.

Make that *almost* everybody.

"Look, Kenny was stupid enough to go running off by himself during a hurricane," Angela declared, her voice

obnoxiously loud. "Why should any of us risk our lives trying to find him? I say he's on his own."

Macy let out an audible gasp. "How can you say that?" she cried, shocked out of her usual cautious shyness. "He's just a little kid!"

"Yeah," Angela shot back. "A totally reckless little kid who doesn't have the sense of a half-witted choo-choo bug."

All the convoluted emotions tumbling around inside me coalesced into simple white-hot fury. "How dare you?" I shrieked, leaping to my feet and clenching my hands at my sides to stop myself from throttling her. "Nobody insults my brother like that!"

"Except you," Angela pointed out, dangerously calm. "Constantly."

I opened my mouth to respond, then snapped it shut again. I didn't have time for a fight with the Evil One at the moment. Spinning on my heel, I headed toward the cave entrance.

"Where are you going, Dani?" Cassie called anxiously.

I didn't glance around as I answered grimly. "To find Kenny."

"Wait!" Josh leaped after me, grabbed my arm, and

spun me around. "Just stop and think about this for a minute, okay?"

"Yeah," Chrissie added. "For all we know, he got bored and wandered off during the dance and fell asleep in one of the caves. He could be there, safe and dry, right now!"

Ryan nodded. "Josh and I couldn't see all that well out there even with our flashlights," he said. "And Ken's a pretty small little dude. We totally could have missed him. And the storm's so loud he might not have heard us calling him."

"They're right," Brooke added in her most mature and reasonable listen-to-me voice. "In any case, it's not safe to go wandering off into the jungle right now."

Even Macy nodded at that. "Don't worry, Dani," she said in a slightly shaky voice. "Kenny's a smart kid. He probably found somewhere safe to ride out the storm."

I hesitated, almost losing my nerve as I glanced outside. The wind was howling more savagely than ever, and the rain was still coming down in sheets. Thunder rolled almost continuously, sounding like a giant's bowling alley directly over our heads, while alarming creaking and cracking noises drifted into the cave from the direction of the jungle.

Castaways

Then I pictured Kenny's grubby little face, terrified and alone. That gave me back my courage.

"Sorry," I choked out, grabbing the wet flashlight out of Ryan's hand. "I've got to go."

Before they could stop me, I plunged out into the storm. As I paused just outside the cave, trying to adjust to the pounding rain and get my bearings, I felt, rather than heard, someone leap forward to stand beside me.

I blinked my eyes rapidly, trying to see who had followed me outside. "Give it up!" I shouted over the wail of the wind. "I'm going, and you won't change my mind!"

A second flashlight flicked on, showing the identity of the person beside me. It was Josh.

"I'm coming with you!" he shouted back.

Ten

I stared at him in amazement. He looked determined. He also looked wet.

"Really?" I hardly dared to believe he was really willing to help. I'd known he was an incredible guy, but this was ridiculous!

He nodded. I smiled at him, more relieved than I wanted to admit.

"Cool," I said. "Okay, let's—"

"Stop!" another voice shrieked over the sound and fury of the storm. Angela burst out of the cave and grabbed

137

Josh's arm. "Josh, don't go!" she cried with a dramatic sob. "Please, please don't go!"

Josh shook her off without a glance. "Come on, Dani," he shouted. Bending against the force of the wind, he headed along the cliff wall toward the jungle.

I followed, allowing myself only one teeny, tiny moment of satisfaction when I glanced back at Angela. She was huddled miserably just outside the cave with a look of shock on her face.

That brief, pleasant feeling was soon replaced by a whole boatload of less enjoyable ones—worry, fear, anger, dismay. . . . Why did Kenny have to pull something like this? And why hadn't I seen it coming and kept a closer eye on him?

I struggled after Josh, catching up to him just as he ducked into the treeline. The jungle, usually our haven from the tropical heat and sun, wasn't offering much shelter at the moment. Enormous trees were waving around like saplings in the powerful gale, while leaves, twigs, and who-knew-what-else whipped past as if the law of gravity had just been repealed. As I looked up and around, feeling very small and scared, a large leaf flapped through the air like a monstrous butterfly, glomming

right over my face before I could lift a hand to stop it.

I let out a muffled yelp, scrabbling at the leaf and almost dropping my flashlight. As soon as I peeled it loose the leaf swirled crazily away again, the wind carrying it out of sight within about two seconds.

"Which way should we go?" Josh cried, doing his best to shield his eyes with his hands and making the flashlight beam bounce crazily among the swaying treetops. We didn't really need the flashlights that much anyway—the lightning flashes were almost nonstop.

I glanced at the trail, which looked more like a small, rushing river at the moment. "Up," I called back succinctly, pointing up the trail just in case he couldn't hear me.

A large tree branch crashed to the ground just a few yards away, startling us both straight up into the air. That sort of jump-started us, and we raced through the jungle, our waterlogged sneakers slogging along the muddy trail as we ducked falling branches and swirling debris.

As Josh slowed to help me over a fallen tree trunk, I glanced at him gratefully. It was scary out there, and I was very glad not to be alone. At least if I got conked on the head by a toppling tree or blown out to sea, Josh would be able to tell my parents what had happened to me. Of

course, if he mentioned that it had happened while I was rushing off to rescue Kenny, they might not believe him. . . .

Doing my best to shake off such negative thoughts, I tried to focus on the task at hand. What was it that my basketball coach always told us? Oh, yeah: *Do what needs doing, and freak out about it later.* Maybe not the most eloquent of advice, but it seemed to fit the bill pretty well just then. I also couldn't help remembering something Macy had said to me once or twice recently: *Look on the bright side.*

I gulped as Josh jumped aside just in time to avoid being knocked out by a large chunk of bark spinning through the air like a deadly missile. Thunder crashed overhead, momentarily drowning out the moaning wind and squalling rain. Speaking of drowning, I had to keep reminding myself to keep my mouth closed so the rain didn't blow in and choke me. That wasn't easy, since breathing through my nose with rain blowing up it every few seconds was like trying to snorkel with a leaky face mask.

Yes, it was kind of hard to see the bright side at the moment. . . .

After I-don't-know-how-many minutes of struggling to

stay upright in the slick mud and dodging flying rubble, we reached a fork in the path. Josh skidded to a stop and glanced at me, squinting against the rain and wind-tossed muck. "Which way?" he shouted over the noise of the storm.

I opened my mouth to answer, but at that moment the heavens exploded with the most ear-shattering crack so far. For a second I was positive that the storm had split the sky wide open and it was collapsing around us. I hit the deck without thinking, burying my face in the mud and throwing both arms over my head. As if that would break the force of the entire universe collapsing on top of me . . .

Vaguely I became aware of Josh's voice shouting something nearby. "What?" I cried, pushing myself up to a sitting position and spitting a small twig out of my mouth.

He was pointing frantically back down the trail behind us, his eyes wide and his mouth forming a little O of shock. Following his finger, I saw that an enormous palm tree had just split in two and was now lying across the trail exactly where we had been about eight seconds earlier. The part of the trunk remaining upright was smoking slightly even in the downpour.

Castaways

"Lightning!" Josh cried, the wind still doing its best to whip his words away before I could wrap my ears around them. "Right there! Did you see that?"

I just shook my head and climbed to my feet. Thanks to my panicky nosedive, I was now coated from head to toe in mud. For once I was grateful for the pelting rain, which offered much more efficient water pressure than any shower in the world. Closing my eyes for a second, I allowed it to rinse most of the mud off my face, then stepped forward toward Josh.

Deciding this was no time to be bashful, I grabbed him by the shoulder and shouted directly into his ear so he would be sure to hear me. "Which way do you think?"

He leaned over to reply into my ear. "Not sure," he shouted. "Ken said something about caves. Maybe the zoo is up at Rockville?"

I nodded, immediately knowing what he meant. During our first few days on the island all of us had spent quite a bit of time exploring—partly looking for food and firewood, but mostly just for the heck of it. One afternoon the twins and I had climbed the modest-size mountain that dominated the central area of the island. About three-quarters of the way to the peak we'd

come upon a sparsely wooded, gravelly area dotted with large boulders and small caves, and had instantly dubbed it Rockville. Upon returning to the beach we'd discovered that several of the others also had visited the area, which was memorable since it was in the midst of acres and acres of lush, unbroken jungle.

"You may be right," I shouted into Josh's ear. "I think I remember him saying something about catching mice in the caves up there."

Josh nodded. "Let's go!"

I focused on the back of his T-shirt as we climbed steadily upward through the wildly undulating jungle. It was difficult to keep from thinking about how stupid we were for just being out there. How many times had the local news back home reported on some idiot getting killed or maimed while trying to surf the storm surge or just get a close-up look at a hurricane? Well, it didn't get much closer than this.

Okay, so maybe it had been impulsive of me to rush out into the storm. It certainly wouldn't be the first time I'd acted without thinking things through. But despite it all, I was still convinced that I was right to try. What else could I do?

Castaways

Finally the trees thinned out and the path changed from pure mud to mud mixed with rocks and gravel. A moment later we emerged at the edge of Rockville. The wind was worse than ever up there without the thick jungle foliage to break its force; I had to grab on to a tree trunk just to keep my feet planted on the ground. My shorts whipped around my legs so violently that I was afraid they were going to blow right off. But mortal embarrassment was the least of my concerns. We wouldn't be able to stay up here long—the wind was just too strong.

"Kenny!" I shrieked, the wind grabbing my voice and tearing it away almost before it reached my own ears. "Kenny! Are you up here?"

"Ken! Kenny!" Josh added at the top of his lungs.

As lightning flared, turning the scene as bright as daylight, I spotted something red flapping furiously nearby. "Look!" I screamed, grabbing Josh's sleeve and pointing. "What's that?"

Squinting against the driving rain and holding on to each other for support against the wind, we staggered forward. As we neared the fluttering red object, the force of the gale was suddenly cut nearly in half.

"That cliff!" Josh gasped in the sudden relative quiet,

pointing to the short limestone bluff just ahead. "It's blocking some of the wind in this spot."

"Good," I said hoarsely, glad not to have to shout for the moment. The diminished wind made it easier to move as well, and I hurried toward the red item, which I soon saw was a T-shirt tied tightly to a tree root protruding from the side of the bluff. My eyes widened as I recognized the toy-company logo printed on it. "Hey! I think this is Kenny's shirt. Do you think it's some kind of SOS signal?"

"Probably more like a decoration-type flag." Josh shone his flashlight at the ground near our feet. "I think we just found Kenny's zoo."

Peering down, I saw a bunch of small white pebbles arranged into letters and words. Some of them had blown or washed away in the storm, leaving the message to read:

MC EE Y'S AGICAL W RL O ISL D ILDL FE:
ALL WEL OM

"McFeeney's Magical World of Island Wildlife: All Welcome," Josh translated slowly.

Castaways

I nodded, suddenly feeling a little choked up. All welcome. "He kept trying to get me to come up here and see it," I said numbly. "I guess he was really excited about it."

Suddenly I flashed back to the museum I'd created when I was about Kenny's age. I'd spent hours and hours putting it together in the basement rec room. It was really just a collection of my toys and various knick-knacks from around the house, sitting on an old ladder, but to me it seemed as wonderful and magical as the Smithsonian or something. When it was finished, I'd convinced a bunch of the neighborhood kids to come see it, charging them each a quarter for admission. I'd proudly acted as tour guide, then sat back to await their praise. Instead the other kids had made fun of it, calling me a dork and demanding their money back. A couple of them even wanted *me* to pay *them* a quarter for wasting their time. That had hurt. A lot. It was only when my parents came downstairs to see, and acted as if the museum was the most amazing, creative, incredible thing that any kid had ever done, that I started to feel better again.

I gulped, suddenly picturing Kenny sitting up here on the mountain all alone just wishing someone would

come see his little zoo. I never really thought of him as having feelings—not like a regular person, anyway. Was it possible that I was wrong? Or were my fear and exhaustion just making me weak in the head?

Josh was poking around in the sheltered area in front of the bluff. "This looks like it might have been a little cage type of thing," he said, gesturing to a jumble of short twigs wrapped with twine. "And here—this circle of rocks would've kept in a turtle or something, maybe."

A quick glance around was all it took to see that he was right. We'd reached our goal. Everywhere around us was the storm-tossed evidence of Kenny's amateur zoo, even though whatever animals had once been contained in the cages and pens were currently nowhere in sight.

There was one problem. Kenny was nowhere in sight either.

"Kenny! Where are you?" I shouted in frustration. He had to be here. He had to be!

My only answer was a sharp crack of thunder and a slight increase in the wind. A large branch blew by about a foot overhead. "Come on," Josh said, looking grim. "Let's get under cover and figure out what to do."

Glancing across the rocky clearing, I spotted a short,

wide opening between two huge boulders. "Looks like a cave over there," I said, pointing.

Josh nodded. "Let's go." We both took a deep breath and ran for it, ducking our heads against the renewed fury of wind and rain as we left the meager shelter of the bluff.

The wind almost knocked me into one of the boulders, but I managed to catch myself with one elbow and shove past it. I fell forward onto hard ground beyond, bumping my head on something directly ahead.

"Ouch!" I yelped, dropping my flashlight.

I scrabbled for the light with one hand and rubbed my temple with the other as Josh appeared beside me. He shone his flashlight around.

"Hmm," he said. "Not much of a cave."

I guess the little hole in the mountain would qualify as a cave, but just barely. I soon realized I'd bumped my head on the back wall, which was only a few feet from the entrance. The entire cave was maybe twelve or fifteen square feet total—smaller than my closet back home. Shorter, too. When I found my flashlight and pointed it upward, I saw that I'd better not try to stand up unless I wanted to add to my head-bump collection.

"At least it's dry in here," I pointed out, trying to look

on the bright side. "Those big, fat rocks out there at the entrance must keep the rain from blowing in." I shone my flashlight at the ground, which was hard-packed dirt with a few little white things scattered here and there. At first I thought they were shells or pebbles, but when I took a closer look, I quickly realized they were tiny, clean-picked bones. With a shudder, I decided not to think about that. I had enough to worry about as it was.

Josh was peering out at the storm. "Looks like we have three options," he said. "We can stay here and ride out the storm, we can go back out and look for a bigger cave, or we can make a run for it back down to the beach. What do you think?"

"What about Kenny?"

In the thin glow of our flashlights, Josh's expression was worried. "I—I don't know, Dani," he said. "I guess he's not up here after all."

"This is all my fault," I moaned, my heart sinking as I tried not to imagine all the terrible things that might have happened to my little brother. "I should have kept an eye on him. He may be a brat and a pain in my behind most of the time, but that doesn't mean I wanted *this* to happen."

"Dani—," Josh began.

"I mean, how hard would it have been for me to pay a little more attention to him after the shipwreck?" I exclaimed, throwing my hands in the air and accidentally scraping my knuckles on the cave wall. I ignored the pain. It was only what I deserved, after all. "I must be the most horrible sister in the world. Poor Kenny. When Mom and Dad find out about this, they'll probably—"

"Dani!" Josh's voice was sharper this time. "Knock it off!"

I blinked at him, startled out of my own despair. "Huh?"

"Sorry." Josh managed to look sympathetic and stern at the same time. "But we don't have time for this right now." He gestured toward the cave entrance. "It looks like the rain's slowing down a little. If we want to make it back to camp, we should go now."

"Oh." Swallowing hard, I realized he was right. The pounding of the rain outside did sound a little lighter. And I would have plenty of time to blame myself later. Possibly the rest of my life. "Okay. I guess."

We scooted to the front of the cave. Even those few minutes of being dry and out of the wind made the idea of going back out there even worse. But I steeled myself for the dash back down the mountain.

Weather's Here, Wish You Were Great

"Ready?" Josh asked.

I nodded, creeping a little farther forward until I was crouched between the two giant boulders that flanked the cave entrance. The air was especially still there. Clutching my flashlight, I took a few deep breaths.

"Okay," I said. "Let's—wait!"

"Huh?" Josh, who was a little ahead of me, glanced back in confusion. "What are we—"

"Quiet!" I pleaded, straining my ears desperately. Were my ears or the storm playing tricks on me, or had I just heard the thin, distant call of a human voice?

"Dani! Dani!"

Josh gasped. "Did you hear that?"

Instead of answering, I dropped my flashlight and cupped both hands around my mouth. *"Kenny!"* I shouted at the top of my lungs.

"Dani! Over here!"

"Okay, that's helpful," I muttered. But my heart was pounding with excitement. "It's Kenny," I exclaimed to Josh, grabbing my flashlight. "Come on, we've got to find him!"

Plunging back out into the storm without a second thought, I stared around wildly, hardly noticing the sting

of the rain on my face. Once back out in the wind, it was impossible to hear much of anything else.

Josh grabbed my arm. "Which way do you think his voice was coming from?" he shouted.

I shrugged. "We'll just have to look around, I guess."

A sudden gust whipped the words away so quickly I wasn't sure he'd heard them. But he nodded, seeming to understand.

The next ten minutes seemed to last a million years. I struggled over boulders and poked my head into caves, skinning my knees on the gravel and scraping my hands raw on the rough stone. Each time I found another small cave opening I aimed my flashlight in hopefully, praying to see Kenny's familiar face staring back at me. But each time I was disappointed.

Eventually I started to wonder if I'd just imagined hearing my brother's voice. Had Josh really heard it too, or was he just humoring me? *Don't upset the crazy girl*, I imagined him thinking. *Just play along, and maybe she won't freak out and . . .*

"*Dani!*"

I was standing near the middle of the clearing, wondering which direction to go next, and the voice had

come from somewhere very close by. "Kenny?" I shrieked. "Where are you? Kenny?"

"*I'm in here!*" Kenny's voice replied, sounding distressingly weak. "*Down in this stupid cave!*"

Wrinkling my forehead in confusion, I glanced around wildly. His voice seemed to be drifting up from the ground directly under my feet. But there was no cave entrance within ten yards.

"Yo, Josh!!" I shouted, waving my arms over my head, then ducking as a large chunk of driftwood blew by.

Josh glanced up from checking a cave across the clearing. A moment later he was at my side. Shouting into his ear, I explained the situation.

He looked around. "Did you check those caves over there yet?" he shouted, pointing to a couple of black holes in the rock about ten yards away.

I shook my head. "But I heard him right here!" I protested.

Maybe he didn't hear me, or maybe he was ignoring me. Either way, he was already hurrying off toward the caves he'd pointed out. With a shrug I followed. What else was I going to do—dig a hole in the rocky ground with my hands?

Castaways

When I got closer, I saw that the holes were entrances to small caves. A third hole was now visible nearby, though it appeared to be nothing more than a narrow fissure in the rock. Peering over Josh's shoulder, I found that cave number one was a broad, shallow opening filled with rainwater.

"Kenny?" I called uncertainly. My voice echoed back at me, bouncing off the still water.

"He's not in here," Josh said, his voice equally echoey.

Backing out, we poked our heads and flashlights into the other cave. It was also filled with water, and also empty.

As I looked around for option C, I once again noticed the crevice near the two watery caves. For some reason Ms. Watson's favorite lecture about being thorough popped into my head, and I stepped toward it.

"Forget it," Josh called, already heading toward another group of caves a little farther away. "That one's not big enough."

He was right. I was sure he was right. Still, I took another step forward. "I'm just going to—"

"Dani!"

The voice was louder this time. I gasped. "Kenny!"

I flung myself to the ground. Ignoring the sharp stones

154

poking into my stomach, I stuck my head and flashlight into the crevice opening.

The first thing I saw was water. Lots of water. The area just inside the opening was little more than a crawl space, maybe three feet high and equally wide. The rocky floor sloped down rapidly in a sort of ramplike tunnel, opening after a couple of yards into what appeared to be a much larger cave than any we'd seen in the area so far. Rain was pouring down the tunnel, gushing into the pool of water that was rapidly filling the main part of the cave. The water was churning inside the cave, small waves lapping against the tunnel and walls.

And there, desperately trying to keep his head above the waves as he treaded water, was Kenny!

Eleven

"Kenny!" I shrieked.

"Dani! Help me!" Kenny sounded breathless. And scared. "Every time I try to climb out of here, I slip back down."

I glanced down at the tunnel floor, which suddenly looked way too much like a water slide. "Hold on," I yelled back, trying to sound reassuring and pretty much failing miserably. "We'll get you out in a sec."

Sliding back out, I quickly gave Josh the scoop. He stuck his head in to see for himself.

"One of us could try sliding down there and then

pushing him back out," he suggested when he emerged.

I bit my lip so hard it hurt, forcing myself to think through the situation calmly. This was no time to pull out my usual persona of Impulsivo, Queen of Leaping Before She Looks. Not when Kenny's life might depend on me doing the right thing.

"No good," I told Josh, holding back my hair as the wind tried to whip it over my eyes. "What if that person ends up getting stuck down there too? That water looked pretty deep."

Josh glanced at the cave entrance. "I wish we had a rope. Maybe we could find a long branch, or—"

"There's no time for that," I said, suddenly realizing the only thing that might work. "Anyway, we don't need a rope. I have an idea."

I dropped to the ground again, wriggling my head and shoulders into the tunnel. "Hang tight, Kenny," I called, the words bouncing off the narrow walls and then the water like a crazy pinball machine. "Get as close as you can to the tunnel, okay?" Then I glanced over my shoulder at Josh. "Grab my legs."

Josh nodded, understanding dawning on his face. "Are you sure?" he asked, sounding nervous. "If my

hands slip or I lose my balance or something . . ."

"We don't have any choice," I pointed out calmly. "Just brace yourself and hold on, okay?"

Facing forward again, I propped my flashlight in the dirt so it pointed downward, then pulled myself a little farther into the tunnel. The floor was slick with water and mud, and for a second I went skidding crazily forward.

Then I felt Josh's hands grip my ankles, stopping the slide. Letting out the breath I hadn't even realized I was holding, I glanced forward. Kenny was staring up at me from the water, still several feet away.

"Lower me in a little more," I called, hoping Josh could hear me.

I felt myself inching downward. Closer, closer . . .

"Dani!" Kenny gasped, stretching his hands toward me and slipping under the water. He came up sputtering and coughing. "I can't reach!"

"Lower!" I shouted up to Josh.

"I can't go much farther," his voice drifted back to me. "Not without sliding down there myself."

I gritted my teeth, willing my arms to stretch just a few more inches. "Come on, Kenny," I called. "We're almost there. . . ."

Weather's Here, Wish You Were Great

He gave a sudden leap upward, scrabbling for my hands. I felt his fingernails scrape about half the skin off the back of my hand, but I ignored the pain as I grabbed at him, latching on to one of his wrists.

"Gotcha!" I yelled triumphantly, holding on for all I was worth. A second later Kenny grabbed on to my other arm with his free hand.

"Dani!" he gasped.

"Pull us out!" I shouted.

I held on tight, and so did Kenny. Josh huffed and puffed and groaned a few times, but he managed to drag us both up and out of the cave.

Once back on solid, flat ground, all three of us collapsed on the rocky floor of the clearing. That didn't last long. As the wind sent what appeared to be a medium-size tree bouncing erratically through the clearing, Josh climbed to his feet. "Come on," he yelled hoarsely. "We've got to get under cover."

We ended up back in that first shallow cave. Even though it was barely large enough to hold the three of us, it was just about the only dry spot we'd found on the entire mountain.

As we all slumped against the back wall, panting and

gulping for breath, I grabbed Kenny tightly by the shoulder. "You little twerp!" I yelled at him between wheezes. "What were you thinking, running off in the middle of a hurricane?"

"It was an accident! I just ducked in there to release my frogs—I figured they'd have a better chance of surviving inside the cave," he babbled defensively. "But then I slipped and fell down into the water. I lost my flashlight, and I couldn't see, and—"

He let out a startled squeak as I impulsively grabbed him in a tight hug. After a second—probably to recover from his surprise—he hugged me back.

Meanwhile Josh was leaning forward and peering out at the storm. "Hey, you guys," he said. "I really don't think it's safe to go back out there anytime soon."

I rolled my eyes. "Duh," I joked weakly. "But when has that ever stopped us?"

Kenny giggled, but Josh looked worried. "No, I'm serious," he said. "It's too dangerous to try to get back to camp right now. I think we'd better stay here until things start looking better out there."

"Fine with me," I said, stifling a yawn. I wondered what time it was, but somehow it didn't seem worth the effort

of glancing down at my watch to find out. Propping my head, which suddenly seemed to weigh about five hundred pounds, against the cave wall, I let my eyes drift closed. About one tenth of a second later, give or take, I was sound asleep.

I was a little embarrassed when I woke up some undetermined amount of time later to find myself drooling on Josh's shoulder. The little cave felt humid and warm. One of the flashlights was propped up on a rock nearby, casting its pale yellowish light over everything.

"You awake?" Josh whispered as I stirred.

I sat up and rubbed my eyes. "Um, I think so," I mumbled, averting my eye from the drool stain on his shirt. Apparently my sleeping self had found the cave wall too uncomfortable a pillow and had shifted onto Josh. "Sorry about that. Guess I fell asleep on you."

Josh shrugged and averted his eyes, looking bashful. "'S okay," he murmured. "I didn't mind."

Kenny was crouched in the cave entrance staring out at the storm. "Hey, you guys!" he cried. "Check it out. The wind is almost stopped!"

Suddenly becoming aware that it was much quieter

than it had been when I fell asleep, I scooted forward to look outside. "Hey," I said. "I think he's right. Maybe the storm is over!"

"No way." Kenny shook his head. "This is probably just the eye of the hurricane passing over us."

"How do you know, you little mutan—" Catching myself, I forced a smile instead. "You know, maybe you're right. It could be the eye of the storm."

For the first time I realized that I'd fallen into the habit of assuming everything Kenny said was idiotic, deceitful, or both. In my defense, a sizable percentage of the time I would be right.

But in this case I knew what he was saying was most likely correct. I'd lived in Florida long enough to know about the eye of a hurricane, that brief area of eerie still-ness right smack in the middle of the swirling storm.

Josh crawled closer to the entrance. "I thought it was starting to sound better out there," he said. "If this really is the eye, it could be our only chance to get back to camp before morning."

Kenny nodded. "But we'll have to hurry. Right, Dani?"

I smiled at him. "Right."

The jungle looked very different as we raced through

it this time. It was hard to see where a path had ever been—everything in sight was now a clutter of toppled trees and scattered branches. Overhead, the dark, angry storm clouds had thinned out a little, allowing the moon to peek through now and then to help light our way. We soon gave up on even trying to retrace our steps, just aiming generally downward. Moving as quickly as possible, we picked our way through shattered tree trunks, clambered over fallen limbs, and tried not to trip over anything or slip in the ankle-deep mud.

Even with the peekaboo moon to help guide us, it was hard to maintain any sense of direction in the weird new landscape, and I have to admit I was a bit surprised when we actually emerged onto the beach only a couple hundred yards downshore from the familiar cliffs. As I stepped out onto the wet sand, a sudden gust whipped past us, almost blowing me straight back on my butt. At the same time, the clouds thickened overhead, dousing the moonlight within seconds.

"It's starting again!" Josh yelled. "Let's run for it!"

We dashed down the beach. Just as we reached the outer edge of the cliffs, another gust roared along the beach. This time the beams of our flashlights picked up

something large flapping toward us. Kenny let out a frightened shriek, but Josh leaped forward.

"It's a tarp!" he shouted, reaching out to grab it just before the wind ripped it past us and away. "Come on, Dani—help me drag it into one of these caves."

"Okay," I panted, seizing one of the tarp's flapping edges. I wasn't really sure why Josh was suddenly so gung ho about saving a stupid tarp, especially when we were so close to home, but it didn't seem worth the effort to argue.

Kenny stopped too, but Josh shoved him gently forward with his knee. "Keep going, Ken," he called. "Tell the others we'll be there soon."

"Okay!" Kenny turned and raced off down the beach toward the supply cave, which was just a few dozen yards ahead. I could see a reddish glow emanating from its entrance, showing that the others were probably still awake and waiting for our return.

I glanced longingly at the cave, then turned my attention back to the tarp. "Okay," I said briskly. "Let's just weight this thing down with some rocks or something, and then we can—"

KKKRREEEEEEEAKKKKK!

164

Weather's Here, Wish You Were Great

An enormous crack of thunder exploded, a sudden garish flash lit up the beach, and there was a loud sizzle from somewhere just a short distance into the jungle. "Yikes!" I shrieked. "Come on, forget the tarp. Let's run for it!"

"Wait!" Josh dropped the tarp and grabbed my hand. "Over here—it's closer!"

I allowed him to drag me toward a nearby opening. A second later we found ourselves in a cave about the size and shape of a school bus. It had a dry, sandy floor and a craggy, batless ceiling.

Shaking the water out of my hair, I stared out at the driving rain. "Why didn't you want to run back to the supply cave?" I asked, perplexed by his behavior. "It's not that far—I'm sure we could have made it."

Josh shrugged. He was pointing his flashlight downward, making it impossible to read his expression. "I just thought maybe we should come in here instead," he said, his voice unusually quiet. "You know . . . to talk."

"Well, I still think we—whu?"

You know that double-take people do on TV when they're a little slow to realize something? Well, let me tell you, people do it in real life, too. Or at least I do.

I blinked at him stupidly. Then I raised my flashlight for a better look at his face. "What are you talking about?"

He squinted, raising his hand to block the beam shining in his eyes. "Okay, okay," he joked weakly. "I'll talk, Officer."

"Sorry." I lowered the beam a little, holding it so it cast a normal glow over both of us. "So what's up?"

Something about his behavior and expression was starting to tip me off that this probably wasn't about the tarp, or even the storm. "It's no big deal, really," he stammered shyly. "I, uh, I just wanted to tell you I think it was really brave of you. Going after Kenny like that, I mean."

"Really?" I shrugged. "It wasn't that brave, really. I just ran out there without thinking. As usual." I let out a slightly embarrassed laugh.

"It was really smart of you to figure out where he was, too," Josh went on earnestly. "You always come up with good ideas and plans like that. I've really noticed it since we've been on this island. Like when you found that cove with all the clams the other day, or the time you figured out how to use the fishing line to slice papayas, or . . ."

I blinked, confused and slightly taken aback by all the compliments. Why was he telling me all this stuff now? It wasn't as if it couldn't have waited two minutes until

we were back in the cave. That way, he could have said it all in front of Angela, too, which would have been a huge bonus for me.

Unless, of course … "Oh, I get it!" I blurted out, suddenly realizing the only possible explanation. "You like me!"

Josh stopped short in midsentence, looking horrified. I gulped as my face quickly turned beet red. Score one for Queen Tactful!

"Oops, I mean . . . ," I mumbled.

"I was just saying . . . ," he mumbled.

We both let our voices trail off and stared at the floor. At least that's what I was doing. I'm not sure what Josh was doing, because I didn't dare look at him. Talk about putting your foot in your mouth—I'd pretty much shoved my entire wet and muddy sneaker in there, and about half my leg as well.

As I was calculating the odds of avoiding Josh for however long we remained stranded, then convincing my parents that we had to move to Outer Mongolia as soon as we got rescued, I heard Josh clearing his throat. Figuring he was getting ready to laugh or inform me that I was completely insane, I peeked up at his face, which was such a deep shade of red it was practically purple.

Castaways

"Um . . . ," he said uncertainly.

There was another long pause. I held my breath, not sure what to do or think or say. If the hurricane was ever going to blow me out to sea, it really seemed like the ideal moment for it to happen.

"Look," Josh said after an eon or two of incredibly awkward silence, "I admit it, okay? I think you're—you know. Pretty cool."

"Really?" I said cautiously. "So are you saying—"

"You're right," he said, blurting out the rest in one long, continuous word. "IguessIlikeyoukindofalotokay?"

"Really?" It seemed to be the only word I could remember. My stunned brain struggled to come up with something else to say. "Wow," I managed at last.

He shrugged, looking embarrassed but also somewhat relieved. "I've wanted to let you know for a while," he said. "It's just . . . I always thought you were cute and stuff. But since we got to know each other better here on the island, well, you know. I realized you were cool, too. Really cool." He took a deep breath. "So, how about it?" he added softly. "Do you think—that is, what do you think? Do you, um, maybe like me back? Or something?"

My mouth opened and shut a few times like a fish gasp-

ing for air. I realized I should probably answer him some-
time before the turn of the next century.

"Uh, umm . . .," I began, suddenly realizing that I didn't
know what answer to give him. All along I'd been telling
the twins and Macy—not to mention myself—that I
didn't like Josh *that* way. But when I opened my mouth
to tell him that, it suddenly didn't quite feel like the truth
anymore. I was so startled by what that might mean that
for a few seconds I could barely speak. "Er, uh . . . I mean,
like, um—uh-huh."

It wasn't exactly what you'd call a coherent answer. But
the last two syllables seemed to do the trick. Josh's worried face broke into a relieved smile.

"Cool," he whispered. "Very cool."

I held my breath as he leaned toward me. My heart
started pounding like a bass drum as I realized what was
happening. I was about to have my first kiss!

I leaned slowly forward, trying to decide whether I
should close my eyes or keep them open. The flashlight
dropped out of my hand onto the sand, but I barely
noticed. Soon our lips were so close to each other that I
could feel his breath on my face. . . .

"Hey!" a loud voice interrupted suddenly, cutting

through the muffled noise of the storm. "Are you guys in here?"

Josh and I leaped apart as a flashlight beam swept through the cave and zeroed in on us. I grabbed my own flashlight to see who had burst in.

Naturally, it was Angela.

Twelve

I first realized I was awake when I became aware of the loud tweeting of birds coming from somewhere nearby. Opening my eyes, I sat up, every muscle in my body groaning in protest as I blinked at the morning sunshine pouring in through the cave entrance. After all that racing around I'd done last night, fighting the wind, climbing over logs, scooting down into caves and such, I was one big ball of aches and pains. Even my little-toe muscles hurt.

A glance around the supply cave told me I was alone in there, and a quick look outside let me know that I'd slept

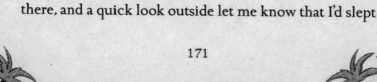

much later than usual. "And no wonder," I mumbled, climbing to my feet. "Who knows what time it was by the time I got to sleep last night. . . ."

Yawning, I staggered over to slip on a pair of flip-flops someone had left near the luggage. After Angela's ill-timed arrival at the smaller cave, she had spent several excruciating minutes babbling at us and fawning over Josh. At least it normally would have been excruciating. Knowing what she had just unwittingly interrupted, I could hardly keep from laughing in her face the whole time.

Anyway, she'd explained how Kenny had returned to home base and reported that Josh and I were still out on the beach somewhere. I grimaced as I recalled how self-satisfied Angela had seemed while describing how she'd *insisted* on being the one who came out to check on us, even though a couple of the others had volunteered.

The three of us had dashed back to the main cave, doing our best to time our run between lightning flashes. It would have been awfully ironic, I remembered thinking, if we'd made it all the way up the mountain and back down again, only to be felled by an unlucky lightning strike on the beach. No, not ironic—what's the other word? Oh, yeah. Sucky.

Weather's Here, Wish You Were Great

But our luck held out a little longer, and upon arriving safely in the supply cave, Josh and I had practically been mauled by the others, who were overjoyed—and maybe a little surprised—to see us back safe and sound. Of course, Kenny had already told them we'd made it back to the beach, but I guess they weren't going to believe it until they'd seen us for themselves. And poked or slapped or hugged us for themselves. And in Ryan's case, accidentally stepped on our feet a few times while jumping around like a crazed monkey.

Needless to say, Josh and I didn't ever get to finish our conversation, not to mention the other stuff. Instead we sat with the rest of the group—me between the twins, him between Ryan and Kenny—and watched the storm for a while. Eventually people started to yawn and wander off to lie down. Ryan ran over to the neighboring cave to check on Mr. Truskey one last time, and I don't know what happened after that, because I was fast asleep.

Forcing my stiff and tired leg muscles to carry me to the front of the cave, I squinted out into the brilliant blue and silver morning. The sun was shining down gleefully, its rays picking out every lingering drop and puddle of rainwater so that the island sparkled like crazy.

Castaways

Not that everything was beautiful, of course. The storm had chewed up the island and spit it back out. The jungle was a disaster area, all kinds of wood, leaves, and other junk littered the beach, and most of our camp supplies appeared to be floating in the lagoon. It was going to take a lot of work to get the place back in shape, and I could see that some of my fellow castaways were already on the job. Macy and Kenny were carefully restacking the stones around the fire pit. Ned was dragging firewood over to the pile while Brooke and Mr. Truskey struggled to hoist a tarp back up over the half-broken frame of the shelter. Angela, as usual, was confusing *working hard* with *hardly working* as she sat on a log and slowly rinsed some sand-pelted dishes in a big pot of water.

I extended both arms above my head, trying to persuade my muscles that all they needed was a good stretching. They weren't convinced, but I did my best to ignore them. My stomach let out an irritated grumble, reminding me that breakfast was way overdue. I planned to take care of that—and to pitch in with the camp cleanup as well—very shortly.

First, though, I needed someone to talk to. The more

my head cleared from its fog of sleep, the more weirded out I felt about what had happened—and what had *almost* happened—with Josh the night before. I'd thought Josh and I were just friends. That was what I'd wanted. Or at least what I *thought* I'd wanted . . . right up until I'd heard myself telling him that I liked him back. And I was pretty sure I'd meant *like*-like. . . .

I sighed, wishing Michelle and Tina were there. But since they were both safe and sound back home in Florida, Chrissie and Cassie would have to do. Maybe they could help me figure out my confusing feelings. Besides, they deserved to know exactly how well Operation DJ had really worked out.

The twins were nowhere in sight on the beach, so I wandered across the sand toward the jungle, figuring I'd probably find them on the path to the latrine or maybe down by the stream getting water or brushing their teeth. As I neared the trailhead, Josh and Ryan stepped out carrying several water jugs.

"Yo, Dani," Ryan greeted me cheerfully. "We were afraid you'd never wake up!"

I smiled weakly. Somehow I hadn't been expecting to see Josh so soon.

"Um, hi," I said vaguely to both of them.

"Hi." Josh stared at me, looking almost as startled as I felt. Then he glanced over at the other boy, who seemed completely unaware of our awkwardness. "Yo, Ry," he said. "Can you take this water back to camp for me? I—uh—want to show Dani that tree with the rock stuck through it."

"Sure." Ryan grinned at me as he took Josh's water. "Wait until you see it, Dani. I found it this morning on my way to the latrine. It's way cool!"

He loped off toward camp, whistling cheerfully as he swung the water jugs in both hands. Meanwhile Josh led the way back into the jungle. I followed silently, wondering if we were really going to look at a tree with a rock stuck through it. That did sound sort of cool, but I wasn't really in the mood just then.

When we were safely out of sight of the beach, Josh stopped and turned to face me. "Good morning," he said softly. "I just wanted to give you something."

"What?" I asked as he fished around in his shorts pocket.

"It took me a while to find the right kind," he said. "The jungle's pretty messed up." I had no idea what he was talk-

ing about until he pulled a slightly rumpled white flower out of his pocket and held it up. "But I finally found this one—I think it's the same kind you were wearing in your hair last night. I thought you might like it."

I held my breath, hardly daring to move as he carefully reached over and tucked the flower behind my ear. As he pulled his hand away, his fingers brushed against my face. We both jumped at the unexpected touch, then laughed awkwardly.

"Thanks," I said, reaching up to touch the flower's silky petals.

He smiled, looking shy but happy. For a second I was pretty sure he was going to make another attempt at that kiss.

Instead he cleared his throat. "Listen, Dani," he said, his voice cracking slightly. "Um, I just wanted to talk to you about last night. You know, when we were talking in the cave and stuff . . ."

He hesitated. My heart froze with terror. This was it—he was going to take it all back. The stuff about liking me. The compliments. Everything. I could hear it now: *Sorry, Dani. It was just posthurricane stress syndrome or something. I must have been hallucinating and thinking that*

you were Angela when I said those things, because she's the only girly-girl for me. . . .

I was so busy concocting imaginary humiliating comments that I almost missed what he was actually saying. Blinking, I tuned in just in time to catch ". . . *mumble mumble mumble* for a while."

"What?" I said quickly. "Er, sorry—water in the ear." I jumped up and down, shaking my head around like a horse trying to rid itself of a fly. After adding a few sharp smacks to my own noggin for realistic effect, I smiled. "Ah, that's better," I said. "Um, I couldn't hear you for a second. What were you saying?"

Josh seemed a little confused by my somewhat spastic behavior, but he obediently repeated himself. "I said, I'm not sure we should tell the others about what happened for a while. The you and me part, I mean," he added quickly. "Not the Kenny stuff, of course."

"Oh." Now I was the one who felt confused. "Um, why?"

He shrugged, looking uncomfortable. "I just don't know if it's a good idea to tell them right now," he said. "I mean, you and I are both leaders of the group. . . . It might seem a little weird, you know?"

Weather's Here, Wish You Were Great

I didn't, particularly. But I couldn't resist his anxious, imploring glance. "Sure," I said uncertainly. "I guess."

"Good!" He seemed so relieved that I was pretty sure it had been the right answer. "Then it's our secret, right?"

"Sure," I said again. Josh was so confident about most things, it was strange and sort of endearing to see him looking so unsure of himself. It actually made me feel a little braver—so brave, in fact, that I was thinking about leaning over and trying the whole kiss thing again myself.

Unfortunately, before I worked up the nerve, I heard footsteps heading our way. Josh and I took a quick step away from each other, and I barely had time to whip the flower out of my hair and into my pocket as Chrissie and Cassie came around the corner of the trail.

"Oh, there you guys are," Chrissie said. "Angela wants everyone to come to the fire pit for a quick meeting. She says we need to discuss what to do about this mess." She gestured at the ravaged forest around us.

Cassie giggled. "Yeah," she said. "Luckily we don't have to clean up from the beach party, since the hurricane did it for us. Unluckily we still have to clean up from the hurricane!"

Castaways

I forced a smile, though I felt more like gritting my teeth. Leave it to Angela to interrupt yet again, even if she wasn't actually there herself.

As we all headed back down the trail toward the beach, I noticed Chrissie shooting me a curious look. When Josh and Cassie took a few steps ahead, she moved a little closer. "Well?" she whispered meaningfully.

I just shrugged, pretending not to know what she was talking about. Belatedly I realized that it wasn't going to be easy to keep my juicy new secret. It was one thing to keep it from a mortal enemy like Angela—that could be almost fun, in a way—but if Josh didn't want *anyone* to know, that meant I had to keep it from my friends as well. And that would be no fun at all.

When we reached the fire pit, Angela was sitting primly on one of the logs. As usual she looked fresh, pretty, and perfectly well groomed. How did she do that, anyway? I was suddenly all too aware that I was still mud streaked and generally grubby from the previous night's adventure. For all I knew, I probably had twigs in my hair and bugs in my teeth.

Macy, Ryan, Kenny, and Brooke were already seated as well. Flinging myself down on the empty log next to

Weather's Here, Wish You Were Great

Macy, I tried not to watch as Josh walked around the fire pit and sat down beside Ryan.

The twins flopped down beside me. "Here we are," Cassie announced to the group at large. "Wait. Where did Mr. Truskey go?"

"He left," Brooke answered. "Said he had a much more important meeting with the broken spirits of the fallen trees. Or something like that."

"Another day, another delusion," I muttered, feeling a little grumpy all of a sudden. Here we were, sitting around the fire discussing Mr. Truskey's lunacy just like we always did. It seemed bizarre, considering everything that had happened. Especially the things I wasn't allowed to tell anyone.

As Ryan dashed off to find Ned, Macy glanced at me, then at Kenny. "Hey, Ken," she said, poking him on the shoulder. "Weren't you going to say something to your sister?"

"Oh, yeah." Kenny leaned forward to stare at me. "Uh, Macy thought I should say thanks. You know, for coming to find me and everything. That was really—"

"No big," I interrupted before he could finish, my crabby mood increasing as I watched Angela stand up and prance

over to whisper something in Josh's ear. "Somebody had to come get you. Next time, be more careful."

Kenny rolled his eyes. "Whatever," he muttered.

Macy shot me a slightly reproachful glance. "He's trying to say thank you."

I shrugged, still focused on the action across the fire. Angela finished whispering, then tossed her head and let out a tinkly, girly little laugh. "That's nice," I told Macy distractedly. "But he's probably only doing it because you talked him into it, right?"

"Nuh-uh!" Kenny looked insulted. "But I guess I shouldn't bother. You probably only rescued me because you knew Mom and Dad would ground you for life if you didn't."

I rolled my eyes. "Whatever, twerp," I said. "Go jump in a—" Suddenly the image of him treading water in the dark underground pond popped into my head, and I stopped myself short. "Go kiss a sand crab," I finished lamely. No matter how much he irritated me, I wasn't ever going to forget how it felt when I wasn't sure I'd ever see him again. Maybe thinking about that when he was at his most annoying would even stop me from wanting to kill him.

I forgot about Kenny as Ned and Ryan turned up and

the meeting started. I had much more important things to think about—like how I was going to keep quiet about me and Josh. Why did it have to be a secret, anyway? Sure, it would be a little embarrassing to have everyone find out we were sort of a couple now. But we would get over that. And it would be so satisfying to see Angela's reaction. . . .

As the others discussed the immense cleanup task that lay ahead, I thought about trying to pull Josh aside for another quick discussion. Maybe I could change his mind about the whole secrecy thing.

Then again, maybe not. Sneaking a peek at him, I wondered if he would get mad if I brought it up. Usually I wasn't afraid to speak my thoughts to anybody at any time, no matter what anybody else thought. But this was different. What if he decided I was just too much trouble? Maybe it was better just to go along with what he wanted for a while, at least until we both got used to this whole new couple thing. It could be kind of cool, actually—sharing such an important secret. Some people might even consider it romantic. So what was the big deal?

As soon as the meeting ended, Chrissie and Cassie

dragged me off into the jungle. Luckily they were too pumped up by all the recent excitement to notice that I was in a quiet and sort of weird mood.

"Finally!" Cassie exclaimed when we reached our private spot near the stream. At least I think that's where we were. Like the rest of the jungle, it looked a lot different that morning. "We've been dying to talk to you about the dance!"

"Yeah," Chrissie agreed. "Not to mention what happened afterward. How totally gallant was it of Josh to rush out of the cave to help you find Kenny?"

"I know!" Cassie cried, putting one hand over her heart. "I almost died when he went dashing out of the cave after her. It was like something in a movie!"

"Yeah, and you should have seen Angela. She was so mad she was practically spitting after you guys left." Chrissie grinned at me. "So what happened out there, anyway? Was he totally amazing and noble and stuff?"

I shrugged, averting my eyes from their curious gazes by pretending to watch a colorful bird flitting through the trees. "I guess," I said. "To tell the truth, I was too busy trying to, like, stay alive and stuff to pay much attention to that kind of thing."

Weather's Here, Wish You Were Great

They both looked disappointed. "So you didn't get to try out any of our flirting tips?" Chrissie asked.

"Sorry." I kept my eyes trained on the bird.

Cassie sighed loudly. "Oh, well," she said. "At least you got to dance with him for a few minutes last night. That's one step in the right direction, right?"

"Sure," Chrissie said glumly. "Too bad Angela got to dance with him, like, twice as long. Knowing her, she'll totally use that to her advantage somehow. Probably by reminding him of it every two seconds and flirting her face off."

"Yeah." Cassie sighed again. "I noticed she's been all over him this morning already."

They both looked so miserable that guilt washed over me. "Look, you guys," I said impulsively. "The truth is . . ."

I snapped my jaw shut just in time. My face turned pink as I realized I'd been on the verge of blurting out the real story from last night. But I couldn't do that; I had to keep my big mouth under control for a change. If Josh didn't want to tell anyone yet about our new relationship—or whatever you wanted to call it—then I was going to do my best to respect his wishes.

"What?" Chrissie asked. "The truth is, what?"

Castaways

I smiled weakly. "Um, the truth is, Angela can flirt her face and both her shoulders off, and she'll still be a dork," I covered lamely. "Anyway, speaking of the Evil One, we should probably get back out there before she feeds us to the choo-choo bugs for not doing our cleanup chores."

"Yeah, guess you're right," Cassie murmured sadly. "Let's go."

As we emerged onto the beach, I felt my new resolve weaken slightly. Angela and Josh were down by the water. She was giggling and kicking water playfully at him as he rinsed a couple of life preservers in the surf.

I sighed. Keeping my word sounded totally noble and virtuous when it was all theoretical. But it wasn't going to be easy to bite my tongue and watch Evil Angela flirt shamelessly with Josh, unable to do anything but grit my teeth and curse her name.

Then again, who ever said being a castaway was easy?

"Come on," I told the twins grimly, turning away from the nauseating sight down in the surf. "Let's get to work."

The End

(for the moment . . .)